GREEN GROWS THE VINE

Three pretty girls sat in the train which tore through the deserts west of Sydney. They could have little idea of the effect the next two months spent at the grape-picking centre of Vindura, South Australia, were to have on each of their lives. For Mitch, just married and very much in love, this was a chance to escape in-laws and to save money for the house which might save her marriage. Maria had married by proxy; but on arriving in Australia from Italy two months before, she had found her Mario dead—killed, ironically enough, on the very motor-bike which had spelled prosperity to him. Vindura was to offer Maria another chance of love, which it would need courage and confidence to take. Mandy was a beautiful girl and a rich and spoiled one. Love had been easily found in the past, but it had always been overlaid with a vanity and a sense of victory. Now, for the first time, she knew what love could mean and discovered the need for sacrifice and unselfishness.

GREEN GROWS THE VINE

Nancy Cato

080611/F

CHIVERS PRESS
BATH

First published 1960
by William Heinemann Ltd
This Large Print edition published by
Chivers Press
by arrangement with
Judy Piatkus (Publishers) Ltd
1987

ISBN 0 86220 213 2

British Library Cataloguing in Publication Data

Cato, Nancy
  Green grows the vine.—(The Windsor
  selection).
  I. Title
  823[F]   PR9619.3.C394

  ISBN 0–86220–213–2

For Eldred: because he is mad also

GREEN GROWS THE VINE

CHAPTER ONE

Iram indeed is gone with all its Rose,
And Jamshyd's Sev'n-ring'd Cup where no one
  knows;
But still the Vine her ancient Ruby yields,
And still a Garden by the Water blows.

'But why didn't somebody tell me?' cried Mitch. 'I mean, here we are only a hundred miles from the city and we're in real desert country . . . sand and saltbush. It's bloody marvellous!'

Her friend shook her fair head reprovingly and glanced at the third occupant of the compartment, a dark girl who sat in the far corner absorbed in a piece of knitting. Occasionally she looked up with a solemn, inquiring, or startled expression. She had refused, with a restrained smile and a shake of the head, the offer of a drink of tea from their thermos-flask. So far she had not spoken.

'Anyone could do a perish out there, I bet—that is, if there wasn't a railway-line,' said Mitch. 'Ruddy miles of it, and not a living thing to be seen . . .'

'Except a few dozen sheep and a couple of kangaroos,' said Mandy.

'Where? Oh, those? Well, I suppose there are waterholes and dams and things, if you know where to look, but still . . . Listen to that!'

A weird groaning shriek came from under the train. The dark girl looked across at the others with wide, startled eyes of a most luminous brown.

'Bunyips! Or perhaps dingoes,' said Mitch,

1

grinning at her wickedly.

'It is sand on the track,' said Mandy.

'It is a very 'orrible noise,' said the dark girl, with a slight foreign accent, a rather too-precise intonation.

Pale orange-coloured sand began to seep in through the cracks of the closed windows. The compartment was hot, the leather seats stuck clammily to their clothes. Mitch's soft brown curls clung damply to her forehead.

She looked across at Mandy, who never appeared hot, and tried to imagine her as a grape-picker, covered in dust and sweat and grape-juice, her hair untidy, her hands dirty. She could not imagine it. Mandy had beautiful nails, unpainted, rather long, and the strong, flexible, shapely hands of a pianist. Her hair was thick, fine and gleaming, falling in a smooth helmet or bell about her face, like metal; a sun-bleached gold on top, but with strands of light brown showing underneath, like a paddock of wheat-stubble at the end of summer.

But there was determination in her strong nose and firmly rounded chin. Yes, Mandy would keep at it as long as she herself did; the amazing thing was that she had ever agreed to come.

It was reaction, of course; the rebound from yet another wild and unsatisfactory love affair, the shadow of which could still be seen in her queer tortoise-shell-coloured eyes. Even when they were at school she had been moody and madcap by turns, and by the time she was fourteen had everyone's brother tagging round after her on sports days.

She, Mitch, had never expected to be married first. Nor had she dreamed that only a year after

2

her marriage she would be setting off for a season of grape-picking in an irrigation settlement, leaving Richard behind at his job in the city.

Yet here she was, on the way to Vindura for four months, and Richard didn't like it at all, and his mother was scandalised, and so were his sisters and his cousins and his aunts . . .

It was his whole family she was running away from, not dear Richard. If they'd had a house of their own she wouldn't have dreamed of leaving; but the nicest of in-laws were only bearable when they lived in a different house. Richard was trying to find a home for them, and she had promised to return as soon as he did so; meanwhile, she would save all she could from her earnings as a grape-picker to buy furnishings.

'*Scusi, signorine*, but at what hour do we arrive at this place, Vindura?' The dark girl was looking at them timidly. Italian, thought Mitch, and a fairly new arrival.

'What, don't tell us you're going to snatch a few grapes too? You'll be sorry.'

'We'll be there by two,' said Mandy.

'Snatch—? I do not think I know this word. I am to be a grape-picker, yes, but I hope to pick many grapes, not a few. At home—'

'In Italy?'

'Yes. At Poggibonsi, in the Chianti district, I work in the vineyards. When the grape harvest is over, I make the reeds into bottle-covers for the Chianti bottles. I have not before picked currants and sultanas.'

'It's simple,' said Mitch, her eyes very bright but her mouth straight. 'The only thing is the grapes are not crushed, so they have to be picked carefully,

3

one at a time, without any stems.'

'One grape at a time! *Veramente?*'

'Now pull her other leg,' said Mandy. 'Don't listen to this menace; she's mad. How long have you been in Australia?'

'I have come *tre*—three months ago.'

'You speak English very well. It takes longer to learn Australian.'

'But the Australian people speak English?'

'Some do.'

'And will there be any wild aborigines where we are going?'

'Never a one. You might see a tame one in the town, or in a humpy along the river,' said Mitch.

'A humpy is a hut,' said Mandy. 'A *casa—casa piccola.*'

'Ah, you speak Italian? *Parlate Italiano?*'

'A little . . . I learnt singing, you see.'

'Oh, *si si*. You like the opera?'

'Puccini. Donnizetti. Some of Verdi.'

'And you know *La Gioconda,* yes?'

'Ah *c'è bella*! And do you know Lorenzo's song?' And she sang, with the accompaniment of clicking wheels and screeching sand:

> '*Quant'è bella giovenezza*
> *che si fugge tuttavia!*
> *Chi vuol esser' lieto, sia:*
> *di doman non c'è certezza . . .*'

'*Brava!* That is good! It is a gay song, and yet it is sad. It is true that youth flies away . . .' Her dark eyes filled with tears; she turned away to the window. Mitch and Mandy looked at each other uncomfortably, and then stared out of the other

4

window.

Now an indigo line of trees was visible above the red sand, marking the line of the river. They had already crossed it once, at The Bridge, where there were 'refreshments'—those sandwiches peculiar to Australian railway stations: large, thick, three-cornered and curling at the edges with the heat. The only alternative had been pies and pasties.

The Italian girl rested her cheek against her folded hands and seemed to sleep. There was serenity in her brow, her full white lids, her dark eyelashes lying on her olive cheeks, the classical curve of her lips. Her pose had the tranquil rhythms of a Raphael. Mitch, looking at her, imagined a soft line of drapery about her head, a gold-leaf halo above. Her hair was wavy, abundant and almost black.

Mitch took a pencil out of her bag and began to sketch inside the cover of a book, capturing the pose in clear flowing outlines. The girl seemed to sense her scrutiny, and opened her eyes.

'Oh, don't move!' begged Mitch.

The girl smiled sleepily. 'So, you are an artist?'

'No, I'm not; but I sometimes get an urge to sketch something—a tree, a face, a line of hills. I always carry a pencil about with me.'

When she shut the cover of the book and looked up, she started forward with her nose against the window.

'Green!' she cried. 'Doesn't it look strange in this landscape? I mean it's so very green, not like gum-tree green which is more olive or blue. It must be vines—we're nearly there.'

While the others gathered their things Mitch continued to stare. It was miraculous, this growth of verdure in the midst of the red sandy plain. They were passing now between wheeling rows of vines, dark plantations of orange trees, green apricots and pears. Poplar trees stood above the level fields and the galvanised-iron roofs of drying-racks. Between the green vines the soil was a rich red.

'You'd better stick with us,' said Mitch to the dark girl as they prepared to leave the train. 'We've got a job with Walton's, the big grocery firm that has an interest in several blocks. On a small block you might cut out before the end of the season. But the manager of Walton's knows Mandy's old man, and we're sweet. Influence!' Her blue eyes sparkled; her thin, eager face was alight with adventure.

Oh, she was glad she had come, whatever her mother-in-law thought—and said: 'Your duty is with Richard ... Really, dear, you seem very anxious to get away from us ... I bought pounds of white wool the day you were married, and you know how I love to knit ... I had thought that by this time ... It is really very disappointing.'

The Italian girl was standing just ahead of her in the crowded corridor, holding her single case, on which was a label saying GENOVA—MELBOURNE, with the name: Sga. Maria Delcalmo.

'Is your name Maria?' she asked. 'I'm Mitch, and that's Mandy Weston ... Mandy, her name starts with an M, too. The Three Musketeers!'

'Don't be so obvious, darling,' said Mandy crushingly. 'Besides, your name is really Edna.'

'Yes; but I prefer to forget it. Lead on, Maria.'

CHAPTER TWO

With me along some Strip of Herbage strown
That just divides the desert from the sown,
Where name of slave and sultan scarce is known,
And pity Sultan Mahmúd on his Throne.

Walton's man was at the Town Hall interviewing applicants for jobs. They had come pouring off the train—new and old Australians, men and youths and girls, following the seasonal jobs of grape-picking, pear-canning, apricot-drying, and work in the packing-sheds of the big dried-fruit co-operatives.

Mitch had spoken lightly of 'influence', but she was impressed by the way the busy manager took time to shake Mandy's hand, adding that if they would wait around he would drive them to their digs on his way out to the packing-sheds.

'I'm going past Block D,' he said, 'you can batch there in one of the huts on a property where we have a manager living. His wife will let you use the bathroom and laundry, and there's a dam where you can swim.'

'Why can't we swim in the river?' asked Mitch.

'It's nowhere near the river. The irrigated area stretches for miles on each side, you know.'

Mitch's face fell about a foot.

She was still muttering when they turned off the road, where the main irrigation-channel was curtained with green willows, into a poplar-bordered drive that led to a low, broad house set in a sea of vines.

7

'Come all this way to see the mighty Murray, and don't even get a glimpse of the river ... Oh!' she said, and fell silent. She had been watching, fascinated, from the back seat where she sat beside Maria (who had been accepted as one of their team), the way the roll of fat moved on the back of Mr Pike's neck when he turned his head to leer at Mandy. 'Leer' was what Mitch called it; she had disliked Mr Pike on sight.

Now she stared at the place where she was going to live, and fell in love with it. The low iron roof of the house, painted a faded red, stood out against a clump of shapely gum trees. The young poplars along the drive all bent their heads one way in the faint breeze, slender and graceful as peacock feathers.

From beside the house the vines stretched away in leafy rows, brilliantly green beneath the blue sky and golden sun of afternoon. For a moment a sense of timelessness came over her. They would forever be moving up this drive, the vines all round, the light just so, that bank of silvery cloud along the horizon ... She woke to hear Maria saying softly: 'The vines—they remind me of Italy.'

They skirted the house and drove along a red dirt-track between the vines. The ugly, grey, one-roomed weatherboard hut did nothing to cure Mitch of her ecstatic state; but she did notice a lack of enthusiasm in Mandy, who was examining the stretchers with an expression which suggested that she hoped not to find what she was looking for, but expected the worst.

*　　　*　　　*

8

When Mr Pike had taken his hearty farewells, they each sat on a stretcher and stared at the others. It was, Mandy thought, rather like the beginning of a long sea voyage when you were sharing a cabin with two other passengers. You wondered if they had impossibly untidy habits or talked in their sleep and whether you would be friends or deadly enemies at the end of it. Of course she had known Mitch ever since they were at school, but had never lived with her at these close quarters. She had always regarded her tolerantly, amusedly and resignedly, as slightly mad. This whole venture had been her crazy idea.

Why on earth had she come? She didn't need the money, and was probably taking the job from someone who did. She would ruin her hands (though she was not worried about her complexion, which retained its smooth golden tan summer and winter), and she certainly wouldn't meet any interesting men in this two-bob township.

Perhaps that was why; she was tired of the endless pursuit, the succession of would-be lovers that followed her like a comet's tail. It had ceased to be important, and had become mere distraction; novelty for the sake of novelty, or for the challenge of a new man who might prove impervious.

She had suffered; she had suffered intensely over the last one when she had stopped seeing him, and it had been more to save her father's shocked bewilderment at the impending scandal than for the sake of the wife she did not know. What 'people' would say had not worried her at all, as it affected herself.

Her mother was dead, and her father never dreamed of the emotional storms that raged round his daughter's smooth fair head. He was an astrophysicist, absorbed in his work and loving it only less than his beautiful daughter. He had looked with a jealous and hostile eye on any young man who wanted to marry her. Mandy now, since most of the men she met were already married, found herself perpetually cast in the rôle of 'the other woman'.

She looked across at Maria, wondering about her romantic life. It was unusual to meet an unmarried Italian girl. They were scarce enough in Australia, and this one was extremely attractive with her pale olive skin and gentle, lustrous, melancholy eyes. Then she noticed the gold band on the third finger.

'It seems I am the only spinster here,' she said lightly. 'I suppose that means I'll have to let you two matrons have the bath first. Mitch,' she said, turning to Maria, 'who was Mitch Mitchison before she was married, is now Mrs Fairbrother. I am only Miss Weston, and you—are Mrs Delcalmo?'

'Yes—that is, I was Mrs, but I am not.' Maria looked distressed. 'You understand, I was married before I leave Italy, how you call "by proxy". I know Mario before he come to Australia. He lived in Florence, and come to see me at Poggibonsi on his scooter. *La piccola* Lambretta! Then, he write to me to learn English, and to marry him. As soon as he saved enough *soldi* for the fare, I come to Melbourne ... and they tell me Mario is dead.'

Two tears glistened in her large dark eyes, without falling.

'Poor girl! I *am* sorry.'

'Hell! What stiff luck,' said Mitch.

'*Deh!* The priest would make you do a penance

10

for that language,' said Maria with a pale smile.

'That's nothing. You should hear me when I try.'

'She has already heard you, in the train,' said Mandy.

'Anyway, let's unpack and do some exploring. We haven't seen the bathroom yet—or the dam.' Mitch bounced up energetically.

The dam, they found, was cemented all round. 'It will be too deep for me—I cannot swim,' said Maria, looking doubtfully at the brown water with rotting gum leaves floating on top.

'Then we'll teach you,' said Mitch.

The manager's wife with her faded yellow hair in a tight bun, was at home. She greeted them at the back door with some reserve, and twittered round them as she opened the door of the back porch that led to the bathroom.

'The floor is only wood, girls,' she said. 'I must ask you not to get it wet, or to dry the linoleum very carefully if you do. That's why we don't take shower-baths; they splash so.'

'No showers—!' said Mitch. 'No one could live through the summer without a shower. You know not what you ask, Mrs Jordan.'

'Nevertheless, I must insist,' she said, shutting her thin lips which were painted to resemble a scarlet thread. 'Now, I will show you the laundry.'

They followed her across the paved yard against the walls of which the vines seemed to break in waves of green; the vineyard stretched as wide as the sea to the flat horizon, with here and there the ship-like mast of a date palm against the sky.

'The troughs,' explained Mrs Jordan, 'are not cement-lined, and I would not like them to rust through. After you have used them I must ask you to dry them as you would a plate.'

'How many times do you like them rinsed?' asked Mitch innocently.

'Once is sufficient. Now, the pegs are never left out overnight . . .'

As they took their leave of Mrs Jordan an immaculately-dressed girl of about eight came round the side of the house. She stopped at a distance and chanted: 'Pooey old pick-ers, pooey old pick-ers!'

'Di-anne, stop that,' said her mother indulgently. 'These girls are friends of Mr Walton's.' She smiled rather acidly. 'The usual run of pickers, you know—! Not even the mailbox is safe from them. I've had half my pegs disappear in one season!'

'Shocking,' murmured Mandy.

As they walked back to the hut Mitch exploded. 'That old bitch hates the sight of us, but she's been told to be polite. Mandy, your old man must own half the shares in Walton's. She's stinking rich, you know—lousy with it,' she explained, jerking her head at Mandy.

'Lousy?' said Maria, looking bewildered. 'Rich? Stinking?' Her face cleared. 'Ah, you mean—*molti soldi*?' and she rubbed her first finger and thumb together, while her dark eyes twinkled with sly humour.

'You've got it, mate!'

CHAPTER THREE

Awake! for Morning in the Bowl of Night
Has flung the Stone that puts the Stars to Flight:
And Lo! the Hunter of the East has caught
The Sultan's Turret in a Noose of Light.

'Oh, what a beautiful mor-ning!' carolled Mitch, swinging her legs over the side of the jinker. They were bowling along the red sandy track beside the railway-line behind a small, shaggy brown horse with the undignified name of Peanut.

The driver was Fred Binks, who occupied a neighbouring cottage on the Jordans' property, and whose wife Rosie was 'boarding' the girls for two pounds ten a week each—that is, she had agreed to provide them with three meals a day for six days a week, including cut lunches. There was nothing in the agreement about the meals being eatable; their first one had not been. The fact that not even Mitch had been heard to make an audible protest said much for Rosie's formidable personality and the intimidating look in her eye.

As for Fred, he looked a villain. He might have been a model husband, a teetotaller, and strictly honest, but no one looking at him would believe it. His face was deeply seamed, his look saturnine, his nose long, heavy, and ill-tempered. It seemed likely that if ever he and his tender Rose clashed, blood would flow. He wore a white athletic singlet tucked into his trousers, and an old cloth cap. A film director would have cast him at once for a part in the chain-gang in *For the Term of His Natural*

Life. He said nothing but for an occasional: 'Gerrup, Peanut, yer lazy bastard.'

Mitch and Mandy were wearing jeans and boys' khaki shirts, and Mitch had a Huck Finn hat of dilapidated straw. Maria had looked rather askance at these masculine garments. She wore a gathered skirt and blouse, a pinafore and a kerchief tied over her dark hair.

A morning goods-train came racketing down the line. Peanut took no notice; the girls waved to the engine driver. Along the railway-line, which was raised above the level of irrigations, the natural vegetation held its own: grey saltbush and blackbush clung in stunted shrubs to the bare, red, sandy soil.

Beyond showed the salt crystals of successive irrigations and evaporations, and then the green began—the almost tropical luxuriance of grass and lucerne and feathery wild asparagus along the head-ditches, and the rows of vines curtained in summer leaf.

A blue crane rose with a scolding croak from where he had been hunting yabbies in the wet sand of the channel. His feet had left starry patterns where he walked. A flock of galahs came over, turning their rose-pink breasts in one flash against the soft blue sky. The air was like a crystal goblet, still ringing from the stroke of dawn.

'*Ah, quant'è bella giovenezza . . .*' sang Mandy softly, and this time Maria smiled. It was impossible to be young on such a morning and not be happy and full of hope.

At the block where they were to work, and where Fred was to drive the cart between the rows to pick up the full tins, they found most of the

14

pickers already gathered round the end of the drying-racks. The foreman was handing out tickets with numbers on them.

'Oh no! He's too much the typical outdoor Australian to be true,' thought Mandy, seeing the long, lean, sun-browned, casually-dressed man in moleskins and faded blue open-necked shirt who squatted on his heels above a tin full of tickets.

He looked up suddenly, directly at her, through narrowed eyes that were keen and quizzical in their glance. They should have been blue by rights, but they were brown, and not a very clear brown at that. But she felt the old familiar shock go through her.

'Damn,' she thought, 'damn! Why does he have to be so attractive? And why should I care? He's probably illiterate, and certainly wouldn't know Bach from Beethoven. A country bumpkin, a—'

'Name, please?' his voice was crisp.

'Oh—Mandy Weston.'

'Miss or Mrs?'

'Miss.'

'Number Eleven. Put one ticket in each tin as you fill it. Any experience?'

'No.'

'Just stand over there.'

He hadn't even looked at her, not properly; she might have been a tree or a stone. Immediately was born the wish to make him look, to be aware of her. Here was the challenge she had never learned to resist. Any experience? Oh yes, but not in picking grapes . . .

Maria, as one who had had experience as a picker, was teamed with a newcomer to the game, a vacant-looking youth with the name of Joe Sloan.

15

Mandy was sent off with Mother Mac, or Mrs MacGowan, whose youngest child accompanied his mother—a small boy of about three years, with snowy hair and a voice perpetually raised in question and comment.

To Mitch fell the partnership of Fairy Smith, an enormous girl who, as she said walking beside her small-boned partner along the row, 'would make two of you easily'. Mitch, looking at the fourteen stone of young girlhood crowned with a mass of yellow hair, wondered if the Smith parents had been possessed of a wild sense of humour, or merely bad luck. Their child was like a caricature of a pantomime Fairy Queen.

The Fairy, however, was an expert picker, as Mitch found when she tried to imitate the apparently effortless way she stripped the bunches of currants from the vine and dropped them into her tin with one movement.

'You pull the bunches back against the way they're growing, and then they snap easily,' she explained kindly. 'Y' don't want to go wrecking yer hands first go by pulling an' tugging. Like this, see?'

'And clean picking, mind—Mike is a stickler for clean picking. Don't leave none behind, and if a bunch of even three berries drops on the ground, you're s'posed to pick it up. I just kick a bit o' dirt over it.'

She crawled through to her side of the vine, taking three empty kerosene tins with her.

'Who's Mike—the foreman?' asked Mitch, tugging at a bunch and feeling the grapes, almost ready to burst with their load of sweet juice, crush into a pulpy mess in her fingers.

Click! Thud! Click-click, thud! On Fairy's side

the stems broke with a clean snap, the bunches thumped rapidly into the tin.

'Mike Hannaford—yair, he's not a bad foreman; a real decent bloke, never goes crook at yer if your tins is a bit light-on. Only thing he hates is to see good fruit left behind on the vine. He wouldn't roust at *you*, anyways; he likes the girls.'

'One of these handsome outdoor types. Not the kind that appeals to me. I always seem to fall for pale, studious-looking types in horn-rimmed glasses; they rouse a maternal instinct in me. Like my husband; he always has a rather lost look, poor lamb, because he's a bit short-sighted.'

'Your husband! You're not married, are yer? You look too young.'

'I'm twenty-three.'

'Golly, I thought you was about sixteen, like me. Is your husband up here too?'

'No, he's back in the city. I'm helping to earn some money for a house.'

'You're on'y supposed to pick through to the wire in the middle, y' know; what's on this side's mine, and on that's yours. But I'll pick through so you can keep up, till yer get the hang of it.'

Fairy was out of sight on the other side of the high trellis of currant-vines, beyond a curtain of green. Only her hands could be seen, picking busily. The bunches hung in tight clusters of tiny globules, wine-purple, wine-red where the sun slanted through them. They were deliciously sweet, with faint overtones of sourness in the skins. Mitch crammed handfuls into her mouth and felt them burst against her palate, the juice run down her throat.

She had begun picking in a woollen pullover, but

now dragged it off and hung it on the vines. The sun was on her back, insistently warm. The thick curtain of leaves under which the bunches hid was wet with dew, and leaves like clammy hands slapped her in the face, long canes pushed her hat off. Her forefingers were getting sore, and there was a crick in her back.

'Try kneeling down,' came Fairy's voice, 'when your back begins to go on yer.'

Mitch knelt gratefully in the soft red sand, dragging the tin she was filling along with her as she moved, tucking a ticket into it when it was full and taking another tin. Fairy kept her supplied by throwing them over the vine from her side. Mitch kept kneeling in squashed grapes, and the currants were beginning to make her thirsty; but she was starting to enjoy herself. She had settled into the rhythm of the picking, and liked the clean snip-snap of the stems, the comfortable thud of the bunches into the tin.

*   *   *

Mandy was not feeling so happy. She was naturally a more indolent person than the small, lively Mitch. The only activity she usually indulged in was swimming, and this she did very well. She was finding the new job hot and tiring; she seemed to take a terribly long time to fill a tin, and she was sure that the forefinger of her right hand was about to break into a blister.

The child, Davey, made things more difficult. 'Don't let him be a nuisance now,' Mrs MacGowan kept admonishing from the other side of the vines; but Davey, who had developed an unaccountable small-boy's worship for Mandy (who was not very interested in children and made no attempt to win him), kept 'helping' her assiduously.

He gathered empty tins and piled them in a heap where she would trip over them; he brought her half-squashed sticky bunches for her tin; he got in the way and asked questions incessantly.

'Where'd you get that watz, Mandy?' he asked, examining the small wrist-watch set in diamonds and sapphires that she wore. 'Is your watz broked, Mandy? Why doesn't it tick? Well, why doesn't it tick loud? What time does it say? When will it be lunch-time? Did you bring some lunch wiv you? What have you got for your lunch? I've got a meranger. They 'quash when you bite them. C'n I help you, Mandy? I'm GOOD at pickin' grapes.'

'Look, why don't you make a motor-car with one of those tins? See, sit in it like this, and hold this bit of vine for a steering-wheel . . . Off you go.'

Davey settled down to making whirring and revving noises, which were less distracting than his questions.

'How many tins y' done?' asked Mrs MacGowan.

'Only five,' groaned Mandy. 'I'll never be any good at this job.'

'That's not bad for a beginner.'

'How many've *you* done?'

'Fifteen. But then I'm picking through; and I've been at this game since I was a kid.'

'Looks like an expert just behind me, in the next row.'

'Where?' Mrs Mac's small, rather withered face, with its dim, kindly eyes and incongruous spectacles on a broad nose ('Like a koala bear in a pince-nez,' thought Mandy) came through the vine. 'Oh, that's Mrs Wilkes. She's a goer, that one.'

Mrs Wilkes was shuffling along on her knees, her arms flailing like the sails of a windmill. Bunches thudded into tin after tin; leaves and broken canes flew as before a whirlwind, and berries fell like rain. Her khaki trousers were stretched tight over a seat of enormous girth.

'She does a hundred and fifty a day sometimes; two hundred on sullies,' said Mrs Mac.

Davey had tired of the 'moty-car', and came back to Mandy, holding a small, struggling ant by one leg.

'Where does the ants come from, Mandy?' he asked.

'Out of little holes in the ground.'

'Where does the holes come from?'

'The ants dig them.'

'But where does the ants come from what digs the little holes?'

'Out of eggs laid by other ants.'

'But where—?'

'Davey,' said his mother tactfully, 'what about going over to the pear trees and seeing if you can find a ripe pear? See them trees over by the drying-racks?' David dropped the ant and trotted off. 'You mustn't let 'im worry you.'

'Oh, he's all right.'

Mandy found herself thinking about the foreman, of his brown hands as he held out the tickets without looking at her. They were surprising hands, long, nervous, shapely as a woman's, the hands of an artist or a musician. Odd . . .

'Psst, I can hear Mike's voice in the next row; he's on his rounds. Any berries on the ground your side?'

'No, I don't think so. In fact, I think I'm being a bit *too* careful.'

She saw the foreman's lean figure at the end of the row, and began putting on a turn of speed, trying to show off. To her confusion she broke off a huge spray, and was guiltily tucking it back in the vine as he came up, bending to look in the tins she had filled.

'Er—some of the fruit,' he said gently, 'is getting rather squashed.'

'Well, it doesn't matter, does it? I mean it all gets dried in the end.'

'Squashed fruit makes sticky currants, and may put the dried fruit down several grades.' He picked a leaf from the vine, not looking at her. 'Also, you're filling your tins too full; the grapes'll be crushed when they're loaded on the cart.'

Mandy swallowed a smile. Surely his studied indifference was overdone? Her spirits rose. 'Sorry,' she said.

'No sense overdoing it.' He flashed her a smile of great charm, so suddenly that she was dazzled. 'You only get paid the same.' He walked on, leaving her with a memory of very white teeth in a brown face.

'He gone?' muttered Mrs Mac. 'You want to watch out for our Mike. He's a bit of a lady-killer, that one.'

'Don't worry, he doesn't appeal to me,' said Mandy coolly. 'Not sophisticated enough.'

'Suffisticated, help! Get the dictionary,' murmured Mrs Mac.

'SMOKE-OH!'

The cry was echoed down the rows. Mandy put a ticket in her last tin and straightened her aching back. Mrs Mac came crawling through the vine to her side, and at the end of the row they came up with Mitch and Fairy Smith. Mitch and Mandy stared at each other and shrieked.

They were coated from head to foot with a sticky mud made of red dirt and grape-juice. There were leaves in Mandy's golden hair, and they looked like the trimmings of a bird's nest. Mitch's dark eyelashes were pale with red dust.

'Why don't youse girls bring your thermos and sit under the pear trees with us?' said Mrs Wilkes, coming up with her strangely immaculate-looking partner. 'This is me daughter, Daisybud,' she added with obvious pride.

Daisybud fluttered her lashes while Mitch and Mandy tried not to stare. Her face was spotless and perfectly made-up. Her plucked eyebrows were a thin line, her mouth was a hard red Cupid's bow, and her hair was pinned into row after row of solid corrugations.

'There's Maria!' cried Mitch. 'Maria, how many tins did you do? How are you going?'

'*Non c'è male*,' said Maria. 'But I only finish one tin. It takes much time to pick these little grapes off the stem.'

CHAPTER FOUR

Oh, come with old Khayyám, and leave the Wise
To talk; one thing is certain, that Life flies;

22

One thing is certain, and the Rest is Lies;
The Flower that once has blown for ever dies.

'No—you didn't really!' Mitch collapsed in the sand, giggling. 'Dear Maria, I was pulling your leg.'

'Come?' Maria looked down at her feet. 'Which leg?'

'She didn't mean it—it was *buffare, burlare*—she was joking,' said Mandy.

'But didn't your partner know?'

'Joe? I think he does not comprehend much.'

Joe was plodding up the row, looking more vacant than ever, when a roar sounded from near the racks.

'Number thirteen! Number fourteen! Who the hell's trying to be funny? Who's number thirteen?'

Maria clutched her tickets and looked as if she might cry. Mitch stopped laughing at once and took her arm. 'Don't be scared. Come on, I'll tell him it was my fault.'

They met Mike Hannaford charging along under the pear trees, his hat thrust to the back of his head, a ticket numbered thirteen and fourteen clutched in each hand.

'Full of ruddy berries!' he was shouting. 'One tin each before smoke-oh! One single, solitary, flaming ruddy tin! Y' wouldn't read about it.'

'Sir, I am sorry—*mi vergogna*—I not understand.' Maria touched his arm timidly.

'You! Are you thirteen? You told me you'd had experience, been picking grapes since you were a child. How do you think we can spread currants on the ruddy racks without any stems?'

'She's only picked wine-grapes before, in Italy. She didn't know.'

He glared at Mitch. 'Then she ought to know. Anyone with a grain of common sense—'

'She had only seen currants in packets, without any stems. And I'm afraid I told her to pick them one by one.'

'Yes, I believe—I not understand it is a joke—'

He looked at Maria's lovely tear-filled eyes and his face softened. 'All right, kid, it wasn't your fault. As for you, Smart Alec, you'd better help her fill her tins for the rest of the morning, to bring up her tally. Don't forget she's on piecework.'

'All right. I'm sorry, but I thought she knew it was a leg-pull.'

'And as for number fourteen—is that him? Oh God, another no-hoper!' as Joe shambled up. 'Who told you to pick the berries one by one?'

'She did.' He rolled his pale eyes at Maria.

'And didn't you think—no, you're probably incapable of thought. All right,' he said wearily, 'you three pick together till lunch-time. That leaves Fairy on her own. Kurt!' he called, to a squat-figured, square-headed little man who came up smiling with square yellow teeth, 'you pick with Fairy Smith instead of on your own for a while. And don't chop her fingers off with those cutters, mind.'

Kurt clicked his razor-sharp secateurs and grinned. He was the champion grape-picker on the block, a Yugoslav who had once had a vineyard of his own in Europe.

At lunch-time they all met again under the pear trees. Fred had lit a small fire to boil his billy, and Mrs Mac jeered at him: 'Hey Fred, you're not goin' to roast us all with yer bonfires again this year! Why don't you get a thermos?'

'Them things!' said Fred scornfully. 'Yer likely to get lead p'isonin', drinkin' tea outa them things. Shut up in a tin bottle all day.'

'They're lined with glass, Freddo.'

'Tea don't taste the same. It's the smoke, and the stewin' and the stirrin' 'er with a gum twig does it.'

'And the ants and the beetles and the ashes and the dust what falls into it. That gives it a taste, all right.'

Mandy and Maria sat with their feet in the dry head-ditch, among purple flowering lucerne and asparagus gone to seed. Mitch leant against the trunk of a pear tree and half listened to Mrs Wilkes' flow of talk mostly about ailments, operations or confinements, about how she nearly died with Daisybud and young Alf had been a twelve-pounder . . .

'Like artillery,' murmured Mitch sleepily.

'Eh? Well, as I was saying, I got this medical book through the post, it's got pictures and all in colour, and it tells you everythink about y'r insides. I said to Mr Wilkes only this morning, 'e was bringing-up again all last night, I said to 'im it's all in this here book if you'd only read it, it'll tell you what's wrong in a jiffy. You know, it's a strange thing—'

'Strange,' thought Mitch, 'life is unutterably strange. What am I, I? Who leans against the tree-trunk, and what is the tree but a collection of spinning electrons, and this pattern of light and shade but the death of the sun, flinging its life away in streaming energy into space?'

'—that's what I always say, any'ow,' Mrs Wilkes was looking at her expectantly.

'Yes; yes, I think you're absolutely right,' said

25

Mitch. She bit into a sandwich in which was a cardboard-like wafer of meat strongly flavoured with garlic.

'I'm as 'eavey as anythink meself, this morning,' said Mrs Wilkes reflectively. 'If anythink was to upset me now I'd 'eave me breakfast right up.'

Daisybud, on the other side of the tree, was repinning her solid curls with about four dozen hairclips. Two loutish youths under the next tree, both wearing artistic orange shirts outside their trousers, were grinning and begging each other to 'get a load of that dame's coyfure', while Daisybud tossed her head with conscious unawareness.

A middle-aged couple came trudging along the cart-track towards the rainwater tank by the sheds.

''Day, Myrtle. Owyer going?' called Mrs Wilkes.

'She's orright, thanks,' said the man.

'Break your fifty yet, Alf?'

'No, 'e only done forty-eight up to lunch,' answered Myrtle expressionlessly.

'That's AlfanMyrtle,' said Mrs Wilkes in one breath when they had passed gloomily on. 'It's a funny thing, but if you speak to 'im, she always answers, and he always answers for 'er. It's a funny thing,' she heaved herself up as the distillery whistle blew, her red, round, lively, inquisitive face beaming like a sun under her cotton hat. 'Come on, Dais. No time to waste.'

*　　　*　　　*

Maria went back to picking opposite Joe, while Mitch rejoined Fairy. In her remorse Mitch had worked doubly hard and Maria now had an impressive line of full tins behind her. These

Australians! she thought, they were really kind but how careless, sometimes, of other people's feelings! If you did not appreciate their rather cruel jokes you were not 'a good sport', and if you were not a good sport you were nothing.

Coming up in the train she had felt a sort of terror; the country was so large, so empty, so inhospitable. There was not even a ruin anywhere to suggest human habitation; just the endless sand and the stunted bushes, among which grazed some queer, dirty sheep looking as though they belonged to the country as much as the kangaroos.

And then, as they drove out to the block, among the poplars and the willows and the green rows of vines, she had begun to feel at home. She missed the hills, the soft blue hills of Tuscany with their neat edging of pointed cypress trees, but the vines made her think of Poggibonsi, of the Chianti vineyards, of San Gimignano with its forest of towers, and Firenze by the silvery Arno where Mario lived, and the flowery hill of Fiesole.

The soft Italian names echoed in her mind like music. She remembered grape-harvests at home, the laughter and the singing, the *stornelli* drifting across the valleys in spontaneous refrains as the drivers of the laden carts answered each other.

And then, at the end of summer, before vintage time, she saw the women pushing their barrows, laden with bottles like green bubbles, taking them home with loads of straw and reeds to weave the fitting baskets that clothed them like a dress. It had been pleasant to sit in the sun, weaving and plaiting and gossiping with the other girls. And then, on Sundays, Mario would come.

Sometimes he took her back to Florence, and

27

they went up to Piazzale Michelangelo and sat on the parapet looking over the slender towers and domes until the sun set behind the hills, and the city just below, with its floodlit buildings, seemed near enough to lean over and touch.

It had seemed the most beautiful place in the world to her, with the wonderful things in the shops on the Ponte Vecchio and the Lung' Arno, even though most of the bridges had been blown up by the Germans. But it was not enough for Mario. He would always be poor in Italy, he said. He had a friend who had gone to Australia and who already owned his own car. So Mario had followed him, and in two years had sent for Maria. First he asked her to marry him by proxy, so that she would be his legal wife and it would be easier for her to get a visa.

And now Mario was dead, killed on the motor-bike he had bought with his first savings. She could not understand how such a thing could happen to Mario, protected as he should have been by her loving prayers. So many *Novenas* she had said to her namesake, the Mother of God, for his safety; and she had made a trip to Siena cathedral to say a special prayer to Saint Catherine, and had lit twenty candles before her shrine. A little photograph of Mario was hanging there yet, in a silver frame.

In Melbourne, where she had left the boat, she had stayed with the very kind family which had befriended her on the voyage. They had an uncle with an *espresso* bar in Little Collins Street, and she had worked there, often very late hours. She would not have minded if it had not been for the son, Domenico, who wanted to marry her and would not leave her alone. She could not forget Mario so soon.

And then, though there were many Italians in Melbourne, she did not like the city. It was too big and noisy after the little agricultural town where she had lived. When she saw in the paper that grape-pickers were wanted along the Murray river, she decided to come. The name of this place, Vindura, had appealed to her; it had almost an Italian sound, and there were vineyards. She imagined that the Murray was a great river rather like the Po, which she had once seen on a summer excursion to Piacenza—a great shallow flood of green water among bars of white gravelly sand.

She was lucky to have made friends with these two girls and to have found somewhere to live so easily. At home, a girl did not travel alone or even go out by herself, and the freedom of Australian girls had rather startled her. But the men were different too, they did not seem to notice girls so much.

This Mike who had been so cross with her—he looked at her in just the same way as he looked at Joe. But he had called her 'kid'. It sounded friendly.

She could hear Joe moving slowly on the other side of the vine, and occasionally his hand reached through languidly to take one of her biggest bunches. She had run out of tins, which were on his side of the row; he was supposed to throw over a supply for her.

'Tin, if you please, Joe.' Silence from Joe. 'Joe, if you please!'

She parted the heavy canes and looked through. Joe's blank face stared back at her, motionless. He was sitting on a tin.

'What say?' he said.

'I say I want some TINS!'

'Oh. Why'nt y' say so?' A solitary tin came over, nearly hitting her on the head. Joe slowly began to pick again, using one hand.

'*Corpo di bacch'!*' murmured Maria. 'He is a *poltrone*, this one.'

CHAPTER FIVE

Dreaming when Dawn's Left Hand was in the Sky
I heard a Voice within the Tavern cry,
'Awake, my Little ones, and fill the Cup
Before Life's Liquor in its Cup be dry.'

Dawn was coming in a clear sky above the long rows of vines. Mitch rolled over in her stretcher, blinked at the different position of the windows' grey squares, and remembered where she was. Twice in the night she had stretched out her hand in the darkness for Richard, and then recalled with a shock that he wasn't there. The single bed seemed small and lonely, the quiet inland night vast and unfamiliar.

An early goods-train came toiling up the line, panting past the house with huge breaths like a tired bunyip returning to its lair. Mitch lay and listened to it, nerving herself to get out into the cold. She had promised herself she would be up to see the sun rise this morning.

She counted ten, and then ten again, and then made a fierce leap and fell back, groaning quietly.

To her surprise she ached all over. All the unfamiliar muscles she had used yesterday were protesting at being made to move at all. Sitting up carefully, she got out at last and stood shivering on the cold, bare boards. Her travelling clock showed just after 5 a.m.; the others would not need to get up before six to be ready for work at seven-thirty.

Should she have a swim in the dam? She wouldn't dare disturb the Jordans by taking a bath at this hour. Nor would she have a swim, she decided hastily, seeing her breath steam in the frosty air as she lit a candle. She was mad to have got out of bed at all.

But as soon as she was dressed and outside she was glad. There was such a tingling freshness in the air; Venus hung in the east like a great silver lamp; and bands of white mist hung above the earth in horizontal layers, like strips of cotton-wool.

It was years since she'd been up before sunrise in the summer. She ran down the track to the dam, feeling her fingers tingle with the cold. The few streaky wisps of cloud in the sky were turning pink, and the dam was full of pink and blue reflections on which the blackened sickles of gum leaves floated. A blue crane was sitting pensive on the windmill platform, and a flock of Noisy-Mynas shouted from bright yellow bills: 'In y' go! In y' go! In y' go! Water, water, water, water.'

'No, thank you; it's much too cold,' said Mitch politely. She stood motionless and watched the little wax-bills come down to drink, calling in their creaking, timid voices: 'What's that? Wha—what's that?'

'Only me; and I wouldn't hurt you,' said Mitch, but they flew away with an agitated whirr of wings.

31

The sky was flushed a pale gold by now with the coming sun. Mitch waited impatiently, feeling the slow turning of the earth beneath her feet, until at last it dipped down and revealed an orange sun, huge, dazzling, like molten metal. Over those flat plains it was like a sunrise at sea. She thought how soon her mother-in-law would be stumping round the kitchen, away in the city, putting on the kettle for the morning tea she could not do without, grumbling to herself in a way that used to make Mitch feel guilty that she should be up getting it instead. Yet the mornings in bed with Richard were precious, almost the only time they had to talk, to enjoy each other's company apart from the family. At night they were always afraid their voices would keep someone awake. Even their love-making was inhibited . . .

Last night she had felt rather lost and lonely; now she suddenly felt tremendously glad she had come. Kicking up her heels like a brumby, she gave a high, wild cry of animal joy and went running back to the hut.

'Awake, my little ones!' she shouted at the two inert figures in the stretchers. 'It is the morn!'

*　　　*　　　*

'Come an' GET it!' Not even distance and air like a crystal goblet could make the voice of Fred Binks sound musical; but hunger made it welcome as a peal of bells. Mitch was ravenous after her early walk, and the others were not far behind her as she shot across to the other cottage in answer to the summons.

There was a plastic cloth on the long trestle table,

32

and three places were set; Fred and Rosie preferred their meals in the 'other room' which was warmed by the wood stove. Rosie slammed down three plates with a sort of fierce pride. She believed that workers in the field needed a meat breakfast, and meat she would give them; no sissy 'cereals' and eggs and that.

The three girls did not waste time eyeing the dark mass of onions and gravy that accompanied the three thin slabs of meat, but fell to at once. Their knives bounced off the meat as off indiarubber. It was possible, they found, to tear it into leathery strips with the fork and so convey it to the mouth, where the teeth bounced off it equally. Still, the gravy was quite tasty.

Rosie came back with a plate of toast, and Mitch said with her most innocent air: 'I reckon this steak came from the Territory, Mrs Binks.'

'Yair?' Rosie eyed her with suspicion.

'Yes; and I reckon it walked all the way.'

Rosie's black eyes flashed a hooded fire. She raised the tin plate of toast as if about to cast it in Mitch's face.

'What's the matter with the steak?' she asked threateningly.

'Oh, it's er—it's a bit dry, I thought,' said Mitch lamely.

'It's very tasty,' said Mandy, swallowing a lump of gristle.

'Hmph!' Mrs Binks set down the plate and, folding her arms over her large bosom under its dingy black dress, gave a silent, intimidating glare round the table, and marched out.

'Golly!' whispered Mandy. 'I thought she was going to take a swing at you.'

33

'So did I. Talk about a she-dragon!'

'I like to have meat,' said Maria. 'In Italy we have plenty of *pasta*, and there is veal, and fish, but not much of bif-stek. There is not so much land as here, not so much grass, and the calf eat too much by the time he grow up.'

'This beef didn't just grow up, it died of old age,' said Mitch, but she spoke in a low voice, with her eyes on the door.

At least, said Mandy afterwards, Mrs Binks made a good cup of tea; but Mitch, who didn't care whether she drank tea or not, remained gloomy. They decided to go into town on Saturday and have a real feast.

*   *   *

When they arrived at work they found that the partners had been re-allotted; Maria was to pick with Mrs MacGowan (and David), Mitch's partner Fairy with the expert Kurt, as she was the only one who could keep up with him; and Mandy and Mitch, to their delight, were to pick together.

'You've got the hang of it now,' said Mike Hannaford to them, 'and you two won't fight over the bunches, I guess. Mother Mac, you look after Miss Maria; Joe hasn't even turned up this morning, he's probably still on the way. He can't do much harm on piecework, but I'll let him amble along on a row of his own. You won't miss him, will you?' he said, grinning at Maria.

She smiled shyly, and the classic melancholy of her face became warm and alive. 'He is very slow,' she said.

'An *andante* movement,' said Mandy

34

'*Si, andante. Cosi.*' And she imitated his languid one-handed style of picking. They all laughed.

'Those things won't last an hour,' said Mike, looking at Mandy, who carried a pair of gloves. 'I'll get you a cutting-knife if your fingers are too sore for picking. Let's see.' He picked up her right hand, casually, and turned it over palm upward. The soft skin of the first finger had a broken blister and a reddened area round it. 'Well! Not much good for anything but playing the piano, I'd say; but we can't have them ruined.'

'They're stronger than you think,' said Mandy. She brought up her left hand and gripped his wrist, leaving a reddened mark on it from her fingers. As she walked away his eyes followed her slim figure, while he rubbed his wrist thoughtfully. His face wore the look she had wanted to see there; he was aware of her at last.

She and Mitch found, as soon as their stiffness from yesterday had worn off, that they were actually enjoying themselves. As they warmed up to the work they took off their cardigans and hung them on the vines. The bunches broke with a soothing snap and they grew so thickly on the vines that they filled a tin every two yards.

The gloves were protecting Mandy's hands for the time being, so that the acid juice did not run into the blister and make it smart. The spirit of competition, which made the pickers dash back to work after each smoke-oh and had little to do with the money they would receive, spurred her on and gave her a feeling of achievement as she tucked into each full tin the ticket with her number on it.

However, by lunch-time she was tired; her back and her shoulders ached, and she got up with

35

reluctance to go back to work when the distillery whistle blew.

The empty tins were on Mitch's side, and the cart came down Mandy's lane to pick up the full ones. On the cart behind the saturnine Fred Binks rode Mrs Wilkes's Alf, in dark blue overalls and a checked shirt, a straw hat on the back of his head. While Fred drove, he cast armfuls of empty tins over the vines, and got down to load the full ones.

The cart came so close that Mandy had to press herself into the vines or be run over. Young Alf threw a small bunch of currants at her, and three berries went down the neck of her shirt.

'Damn you!' she said, clawing them out, and making a face at him.

'Not bad, eh, Fred? Where did she come from?'

'Young women is things,' said Fred, 'that I 'ardly ever notices; but she's one of them we call Pike's Privileged Pickers, staying up at the Jordans' second cottage.'

'Oh, one of that mob,' said Young Alf, and Mandy's eyebrows rose. Evidently the others already had them taped.

Young David, tired of asking questions of an uncomprehending Maria, came down the row in search of Mandy. He was holding a completely bald thistle-head and blowing at it mightily. His pale, straight hair fell over his clear brown eyes. The knees of his little khaki overalls were red with sand and currant-juice.

'Hullo, Mandy, it's one o'clock. C'n I see your watz, Mandy? Wha' time does it say? Is your watz broked? What are the blue 'parkly things round it? What's saffirs? Your watz must be broked, because it isn't free o'clock yet by the fistle.'

36

'Oh, help!' groaned Mandy. 'Can you hear him, Mitch? He never stops for a moment unless he's eating. Here, Davey, have some currants.'

'I've had some, fanks.'

'And I bet *that*'s an understatement.'

'Maria's pickin' with my mummy now, she's good at pickin' grapes, but she talks funny—'

'Ooh, come and see what I've found, David.' There was such excitement in Mitch's voice that he immediately crawled through to her side. It was a pale, creamy-coloured toad. Mitch was holding it tenderly in the palm of her hand. 'Look at its eyes, David. They look as though they're made of gold; beautiful!'

'Ugh, horrid thing!' Mandy put her head through the leaves. 'I thought at least you'd found a nugget.'

David wanted to keep it in his hot little palm, but Mitch crossed to the next row and hid the toad deep in the tangled grass at the foot of the vines.

Mandy drew her head back to her own side and began to pick again, or rather cut, for Mike had provided her with a knife; Mitch preferred to use her hands still. Mandy had already cut her left hand with the knife, so that now both hands were sore, and the currant juice ran into the cut and the blister and smarted horribly. The gloves had worn through in the first hour.

To make things worse, she found that as the day went on and the dew dried out of the vines, the white fluff that coats the back of currant-leaves floated off in the air as she picked, and gave her hay fever. She sneezed and her eyes became reddened and half closed, her head stuffy so that her voice sounded thick. 'He'll never look at me now,' she thought, remembering, however, with a little thrill, that it was down her side of the row Mike had walked when bringing picking-knives. She had noticed today, as he stood beside her demonstrating the use of the knife, how the little laughter-crinkles at the corners of his eyes were paler than the rest of his brown face, for they had escaped being sun-burnt.

He had been wearing, as usual, a battered old Digger's hat, its wide brim pulled down fore and aft into the shape of a boat, but under it showed a careless lock of dark brown hair. The hairs on his forearms were lighter, bleached by the sun. She had watched his deft, strong hands working among the bunches, had noticed again their fine bone-structure.

'Mitz has found a fog,' said David, crawling back through the vines. 'She won't let me keep it. I fink she's mean . . .'

Mandy became aware, from the tingling of her nerves, that Mike Hannaford was approaching, and buried her face in the vine so that he would not see her disfigured eyes.

'You did seventy-four tins yesterday,' said his voice behind her. 'Not bad for a beginner. How's the knife going?'

'All right, thanks.'

'I helped her, Mike,' piped David. 'I'm GOOD at pickin' grapes.'

'Hullo, young feller. How'd you like to come and help me drive the tractor? I've got to open up some furrows between the sullies for the last irrigation.'

'Ooh! The trafcar!' David was swung on to the tall man's hip, and clung there beaming as Mike went striding off down the row.

CHAPTER SIX

Into this Universe, and why *not knowing,*
Nor whence, *like Water willy-nilly flowing:*
And out of it, as Wind along the Waste,
I know not whither, *willy-nilly blowing.*

There was a full moon the next night. Mandy glanced restlessly out of the window. Though she was tired, a swim in the dam, a bath and a change into a light frock had refreshed her. She could not settle down with a book.

Mitch, seated at the one small table, was writing a long letter to Richard; Maria was reading a bundle of old letters from Mario. Both were absorbed, one in the future, the other in the past.

A cloud of insects came in the open windows past the ill-fitting screens, to circle madly round the kerosene lamp and flop upon the table. Mandy opened the creaking wire door and stepped out into a bath of the most brilliant moonlight she had ever seen.

Towards the east, the vines stretched away in misty rows, veiled in a shimmer of light. Westward the poplars were black against the pale, light-drenched sky. The moon was so bright that she could distinguish colours, the ghostly redness of sand, the almost green of leaves.

Life, the secret life of growing plants, pulsed all round her through a million intricate veins. She was a city girl, born and bred among bitumen roads and houses of stone and brick. She felt almost intimidated by the quantity, the exuberance, of

39

green living things called out of the barren sand by the simple miracle of water.

Vine and poplar, banana and date palm, saltbush and gum tree grew together and accepted each other's alien presence; it was she, the separate, thinking human being aware of its apartness who was the intruder here.

She walked along the cart-track away from the Binks's cottage, towards the road, and became aware of a water-music filling the night. The head-ditch was flowing, with a faint bubbling sound as it overflowed into the furrows, and everywhere resounded the joyous chorus of the frogs—deep bass of bull-frogs, treble of little frogs, with the liquid accompaniment of bubbling water.

The irrigation was beginning. Even as she watched, a long silver serpent began to crawl out from the ditch at her feet; beside it, in the next row and the next, another serpent slid forth its head. Gradually the black earth was becoming striped with silver bars.

Water! From the far-away river the water was being pumped out into the thirsty furrows. The grateful scent of parched earth drinking was breathed into the air.

Mandy walked, balancing on the smooth cement edge of the head-ditch, until she came to the main channel just inside the fence. Here the water was flowing like a small river. She dipped a sandalled toe in. Pleasantly warm, not at all cold. Without thinking she slipped out of her light clothes and into the channel, stretching full length with her fingers resting on the cement bottom.

The water was alive, flowing like the blood in a great artery through the body of the land. She felt the moonlight flooding down from the sky, the water stroking her flanks as it flooded out into the vineyards, the orange groves and the pear and apricot orchards to nourish the swelling fruit. She was a part of that mysterious force.

'Eh, wait for us, carntcher?' A nasal shout floated down the road. 'Alf! Wait on.'

Mandy stiffened as she saw the wobbling light of a bicycle approaching, followed at a distance by another. The rider of the first bike was almost level with her as he stopped and rested one foot on the ground, turning to look back.

'Get a move on, then.'

The second bike, with another youthful rider accompanied by a black dog, came up and stopped beside the first.

'Thought it was you, Alf. What's the hurry?'

'Goin' into the dance,' said Alf. 'Mrs Wilkes's young Alf,' thought Mandy in alarm. She submerged almost entirely, leaving just the tip of her nose out.

'Well, so am I. Say, you've got some good-lookers on the block this year. That blonde I saw ridin' on the cart with Fred Binks today—'

'Yair, not bad. But 'er nose is a bit big.'

'Gawd, you don't wanter look at 'er *nose*. What about 'er brace an' bits?'

'Two beauts, aren't they?' Alf picked up a stone and tossed it aimlessly towards the channel. The dog followed, and caught sight of Mandy's offending nose in the water. Whether he thought in some canine fashion that it was a fish, an eel or some such game, or realised that it was human, he began barking madly.

'Come on, Alf, if we're goin' we better make

tracks.'

'What's the matter with that blarsted mong?' said Alf, staring.

'Dunno. Seen a frog most likely.'

'It might be a Joe Blake.'

'Aw, come *on*.'

They set their feet to the pedals and wobbled away, whistling to the dog. It gave a few last barks and left reluctantly. Mandy, shivering from keeping so still in the water, climbed out as soon as she dared and dressed in the shadow of a great poplar which towered above her with softly-sighing leaves. She felt inclined to giggle. She ran back to the hut to get warm and tell the others of her adventure. Mitch was amused, Maria looked slightly shocked.

At home it had been considered immodest for a girl to wear a dress without sleeves. Here she had seen Mandy change after work into a pair of very brief shorts and a sun-top like a brassière, and be quite unembarrassed by the glances of Fred Binks or of Mr Jordan, who had come over to make their acquaintance and to extend an invitation to dinner for Saturday night from his wife.

Though the young people went swimming in the Arno in summer, she herself had never owned a bathing-costume. One of the things they were going to town for on Saturday, Mitch declared, was to choose a costume for Maria so that they could teach her to swim.

*   *   *

'Mitch!' cried Mandy reproachfully. 'You've been shaving your legs in my bath water. As if it wasn't bad enough to have half the silt from the whole of the Murray-Darling Basin in it—'

'Now, Mandy, I've told you a million times not to exaggerate. It's just slightly brown, that's all. And I can't get a pumice-stone for my legs till we go to town, and I'm not going to town with black fur all over them—'

'Oogh, it's revolting. Why didn't you let me get in first?'

'Because you weren't ready, my sweet, and we have to catch a bus, remember?'

'And there isn't enough wood to run another bath. I'm going to have a shower, just a little one.'

'Good for you! The freedom of the individual! Down with the Jordans who would dictate to us! "A little water clears us of this deed"—or rather, a little judicious mopping with a towel will remove the evidence. Sing, Maria, sing! We must cover our comrade's actions.'

Maria, who for reasons of modesty had had first bath and was already in her under-things before the others arrived, piled the last of the chips into the heater. (Having first bath, in spite of its advantages of cleaner water, meant getting the ancient heater to work without it boiling or blowing up, and this was a nerve-racking task.) She averted her eyes from Mandy's long golden shape in the water, and Mitch capering about in nothing but a pair of briefs.

Then, as the heater wheezed and hissed and the water trickled reluctantly from the shower, she and Mitch began a noisy rendering of *Santa Lucia*, Mitch at the same time turning on a tap in the wash-basin and making splashing noises, while Maria beat time on the medicine-chest with a tooth-brush and a comb.

43

'Oh, that was lovely,' sighed Mandy, stepping out and towelling herself with leisurely grace.

'Hell, I wish I had a pencil,' said Mitch, studying her friend's lithe figure with impersonal admiration. 'You could always earn a crust as a model, if you weren't so stinking rich.'

She is like the figure of Dawn on Lorenzo de Medici's tomb in Florence, thought Maria. There was a replica of Michelangelo's Dawn and Night, and of his David, on the Piazzale where she used to go with Mario ... *Caro Mario; ahi Mario, mio tesoro!*

Yet the old pain did not come back when she said his name to herself like that. It could not be that she was forgetting, she would never forget him; but the change, the new life, the work in the open air to which her healthy young body responded, the company of the other girls, had filled her with a new sense of well-being. She was beginning, ever so slightly, to feel at home in her new country.

When, all dressed in their prettiest cotton frocks, hatless hair shining, lipstick outlining the tender curves of their young lips, they emerged from the hut, there was a new light of happiness in her dark eyes. '*Andiamo!*' she cried, leading the way down the drive to the bus-stop on the corner.

In the town, where all the shops opened on Saturday afternoons to give the workers time to do their shopping, she felt even more at home. It was a pretty little town, with public gardens full of flowers and green lawns sloping down to the river; a post office, a railway station, a main street as at home. If only the streets were not all so flat, and lined with such ugly wooden veranda-posts!

On every corner, and especially outside the

cafés, there were groups of young Italian men, with long hair-cuts and smart blue suits. *'Bellezza!'* they cried as the girls walked past, and made hissing noises to attract their attention.

'Ci sono molti Italiani qui!' muttered Mandy in her ear.

'Si, molti, molti.' Maria lowered her eyes modestly.

Mandy looked boldly and indifferently at the groups of would-be swains. Mitch was staring avidly at the river.

Smooth as green glass, still as a lake, the water reflected the willows that drooped their fronds into their own reflections, so that it was impossible to tell where tree ended and water began. Below the town was a lock and weir, so that the river was held back in a still pool. White launches nestled in the willows, a paddle-steamer with passengers on a river cruise was tied up at the wharf, where a group of young people swam and dived. Beyond the wharf was the exclusive, august building of the Riverside Club, and the massive Community Hotel, modern and imposing.

Maria looked about for an equally imposing church or cathedral, but there was none visible. She was struck by the newness of everything, the temporary look of wood and galvanised iron buildings and fences. The most solid-looking building apart from the hotel was the headquarters of the Irrigation Trust set among a grove of palms.

The girls did their shopping (they had been paid that morning, Maria collecting the fattest envelope because she was a faster picker), had a milk-shake, and then walked down to the river. At the gate of the Riverside Club they saw Mr Pike, with an angular matron who was presumably his wife. He seemed for a moment undecided whether to ignore them, as mere pickers, or welcome them, as friends of Mr Walton's.

He compromised with a wave and a condescending: 'Well, girls; getting on all right?' He did not introduce his wife, who stared frostily over their heads.

'We'll probably survive,' said Mandy laconically.

He raised his eyebrows, gave an uncertain smile, and followed his wife through the gate.

'What a drongo,' said Mitch.

'Dron-go?' said Maria.

'A dill—a no-hoper.'

Maria spread her hands helplessly.

'*Stupido*,' said Mandy.

'Oh, *si, si—capisco!*'

As they were to have a free meal at Mrs Jordan's that night, they decided not to eat in town after all. As Mitch said, it would only be a waste since she couldn't taste anything, because the inside of her mouth was still burning from the intensely hot curry Mrs Binks had provided for both breakfast and lunch. Diluted with masses of tomato sauce, it had been just eatable.

They were in high spirits at the prospect of their first social outing, and walking home from the bus-stop they sang, to a well-known hymn tune:

'What's for din-ner, Mrs Binks?
Do you know your curry stinks?'

'What is "stinks"?' from Maria. 'You mean it is rich?'

'You know, pongs. It means something's on the nose,' explained Mitch patiently.

'But before you say Mandy stinks because she is

rich—'

'No, no, I didn't say *Mandy* stinks. I said she was stinking *rich*. That only means she has a lot of money, she's stinking with it. But the curry pongs—it smells. Or rather it's made strong so we can't tell how much the meat stinks. It's probably just about crawling.'

'*Mamma mia!* I will never learn Australian.'

CHAPTER SEVEN

Ah, fill the Cup:—what boots it to repeat
How Time is slipping underneath our Feet:
Unborn TO-MORROW, *and dead* YESTERDAY,
Why fret about them if TODAY *be sweet!*

Much scrubbing with Mitch's new pumice-stone, much painful application of lemon juice to broken skin, had at last removed the grape-juice stains from their hands, and the three felt ready to step out into Vindura society.

'We can't dine at the Jordans' with "pooey old pickers' hands", in case that little menace of a Di-anne is there,' said Mitch.

None of them had anything like a dinner-frock among their luggage, but only Maria was shy about entering the big bungalow-type house, set so solidly among its wide creeper-covered verandas, as a dinner-guest instead of a supplicant for baths.

Mrs Jordan came fluttering out to the front veranda to meet them, in a long floral gown with floating draperies from the shoulders.

'Oh, there you are, my dears,' she said vaguely.

'Come on in—or would you rather stay outside in the cool? Dinner's not for half an hour yet. Bob! Where are you? Look after these girls, will you, and find them a drink? I must just go and peep in the oven.'

Bob Jordan, a large, hearty, sanguine-complexioned man with a complacent expression and a blue-black jowl that looked as if it was never shaved properly, brought them each a tall glass of ice-cold beer. Maria regarded the amber, foam-capped liquid doubtfully, and said she thought perhaps if there was some wine . . .

But Mitch said firmly that if she was going to be an Australian she must learn to drink beer and like it. Maria explained that she liked beer, but she was more used to wine, and that beer in such a long glass might go to her head.

'It's very light,' said Mitch, who believed that this was true.

There were several guests walking on the twilit lawn, from which came a scent like that of mown hay as the dew descended upon the cut grass. Others stood about on the lighted veranda. Mr Jordan introduced Mitch to a fair, breathless little woman in hideously green chiffon.

She immediately began on the favourite topic of the growers' wives at this time of year: the iniquity of the pickers. They'd had two on their block last year who used to get drunk on the week-ends; she didn't believe they were even married, though they enrolled as a married couple. And they would, of course, steal anything . . .

'Yes, I know what they're like,' said Mitch, with an affectation of sympathy. 'You see, I'm a picker myself; so is Maria here.'

'Oh, er, well! I suppose just for *fun*—'

'No, not for fun, to earn money.'

'Indeed, how int'resting!' but she drifted rapidly away.

Mandy, in a strapless, form-fitting dress of yellow linen, cut with a severe simplicity that made the other women's dresses look hopelessly fussy, and with her pale golden hair gleaming under the veranda lights, was already the centre of a group of three men. Her eyes, that were sometimes more green than brown, tonight were tawny as a tiger's. Someone had better beware, thought Mitch, as she smiled encouragingly at the rather lost-looking Maria. Mandy is on the prowl . . .

She set her empty glass down on the veranda parapet, and ran her hand over the red stones, still warm from the sun. Maria emptied her glass too, and said that she liked Australian beer. Mitch lifted her hand and saw that it was stained a dark red from the painted stonework.

Mrs Jordan came up and took her empty glass while she was rubbing uselessly at the stain with her handkerchief.

'That wretched rail! I should have warned you. Go down to the bathroom, you know the way. There's a guest towel by the basin—'

But the moment Mitch touched her hands with soap, they turned a deep navy-blue. The grape-juice stains, neutralised with the lemon, had come back twice as dark at the touch of an alkali.

Meanwhile Maria was in something of a panic, which did not show in her tranquil face and calm hands, only in the hunted look in her large dark eyes. No one spoke to her or brought her another drink. Mandy, a glass in one hand, a cigarette in the

other, was laughing, quite at home, with her group
of men which had now been joined by Bob Jordan.
She ignored Maria, or perhaps had just forgotten
about her.

Maria leant disconsolately on the veranda
balustrade, wishing she had not come, wondering if
she could escape back to the hut. She did not like
this sort of party. There was no music, no singing,
and she did not know anybody. And she was afraid
there would be all sorts of knives and spoons and
special forks she would not know how to use, as
there had been on the ship coming out to Australia.
She felt a longing for a big plate of *pasta*, some red
wine and perhaps a fresh peach to finish with; an
almost physical yearning for the faces, the voices,
the ways of her own people.

There was a movement indoors now, as Mrs
Jordan came out to announce that dinner was
ready. It surprised Maria that such a big, wealthy-
looking house had no servants; it seemed that
Australian girls would not do housework for a
living if there was anything else they could possibly
do instead. They would rather work in noisy
factories, or stand up all day in shops . . .

She was almost alone on the veranda, and
wondering if anyone would see her if she ran away,
when Mitch came back; Mitch in pale blue cotton,
crisp and fresh, her soft brown curls clustered
about her head, her eyes bluer than by day.

'Where's Mandy? Why isn't anyone looking after
you?' she asked indignantly.

Maria stood up from the balustrade, suddenly
feeling that she liked Mitch very much, and not
dreading so deeply the ordeal ahead. She looked
down, and gave a cry of dismay to see that the front

of her white frock was smeared with red powder.

'And my hands have turned blue, now!' wailed Mitch. 'Well, three cheers for the red, white and blue! Let's keep together, mate, and share our shame.'

To her relief, Maria found that it was not a formal dinner-party; it was a buffet dinner, and guests were standing about the large dining-room eating with forks from plates held in their hands. The first plate handed to her was piled with spaghetti in tomato sauce.

'That's the stuff you Da—er, Italians like, isn't it?' said Bob Jordan heartily, giving her a fork.

'Oh yes! But more in the south than where I come from, they eat *pasta*.'

'Spaghetti da macaroni, eh? Ice-a-da-cream.'

'*Si*, but there are many other kinds of *pasta*— *capelli d'angeli*, very fine, that is angels' hair, *vermicelli*, that you call vorms, *mustacchi*, and *ravioli* that is like little cushions—'

'It's all spaghetti to me,' he said indifferently.

'There's that little bastard of a Di-anne,' whispered Mitch as he moved away. The daughter of the house, in a frilly pink frock and with a pink bow in her sausage curls, was peeking in the door. Mitch scowled at her and put one of her blue hands behind her back. Bob Jordan came back with two more glasses of beer. Maria found when she had drunk it that she felt quite happy and not at all frightened any more.

After the meal was finished, she noticed that the party broke up into two distinct groups. The men gathered about the keg on the veranda, and appeared to be enjoying themselves very much. One would talk for a while in a slightly lowered voice, and then all would break into a roar of laughter. Maria supposed it was some sort of traditional entertainment. She had seen the men dancing together at home, or joining in part-singing.

The women sat about the drawing-room in little knots, exchanging confidences and anecdotes, mostly about food, clothes or babies. They did not seem to be enjoying themselves so much, and after one of the bursts of merriment from the veranda would look towards the group of men in a rather irritated fashion. Mandy, looking bored, was turning over some music on the piano.

'Why don't you play for us, dear? Mrs Walton was telling me you play beautifully,' said Mrs Jordan.

Mandy made a little grimace, but sat down at the piano, picking up a volume of Beethoven sonatas. She launched into the *Quasi Una Fantasia*, feeling that it should be hackneyed enough for the present company.

Closing her eyes, for she knew it too well to need the music, she let the notes ripple out from under her fingers, like cool drops of water falling through the night. Skipping the vigorous second movement, she went on to the third, and saw, as always, a small sled drawn by three black horses moving over a snowy landscape lit by moonlight. It dropped into hollows and crossed small hills, following the land that undulated like the music, then dipped into a final valley and was gone.

Mandy opened her eyes like a sleep-walker awakened, and looked round the room. There was a murmur of polite applause, but the groups were still talking. She played a lively Chopin polonaise, and mischievously began a jazzed-up version of his *Marche Funèbre*.

Some of the men drifted in from the veranda. Others followed, and Mandy brightened visibly. She started to play *Santa Lucia*, and for the first time that evening seemed to notice Maria.

'Come on, Maria, let's hear you sing it in Italian.'

'Yes, do!' cried Mrs Jordan. 'I know you can sing it, I heard you in the bathroom this afternoon.'

Then the old bitch *was* listening to see if we were using the shower, thought Mitch. Aloud she said: 'Come on, Maria, I'll sing with you.'

Maria, who had just finished her third large glass of beer, had the strangest feeling of unreality. Who these strangers were, or why she was here, she could not remember; but she felt happy and confident and quite ready to sing:

> *'Mare si lucido,*
> *Lido si caro . . .'*

By the time she had reached the chorus the second time everyone was joining in, loudly if not tunefully.

> *'Venite al' agile*
> *Barchetta mia . . .*
> *Santa Lucia,*
> *San-ta Lucia!'*

By now all but the most determined beer-drinkers had left the veranda, the women had stopped discussing babies and looked less discontented, and the party was beginning to be a success. It was then that the phone call came for

Mitch—a trunk-line call from the city.

She came back looking rather white, and hastily swallowed a beer.

'It is bad news from home?' asked Maria timidly.

'Not exactly. But that was Richard—my husband. He wants me to come home. He hasn't found a house, nothing's changed, but he insists I should give up this job and come back at once.'

'Then you will have to do so, *non è vero?*'

'No! Why should I? I'm earning money for the house, and heaven knows we'll need it. Besides— I'm not going to give in now. "What, without asking, whither hurried hence?"' she muttered. She held out her glass to be filled by a man passing with a foam-topped jug, and drank its contents straight down.

'Another and another Cup to drown
The memory of this Impertinence.'

'You are talking poetry?'

'Omar Khayyám. A wonderful bloke.'

'I, too, know some poetry. We had to learn it at school:

*'Nel mezzo del' cammin di nostra vita
Mi ritrovai per una selva oscura
Che la diritta via era smarrita . . .'*

Maria's eyes were bright; her cheeks were flushed. The words seemed to tumble out of her mouth, but she had very little control over them. Mitch was staring at her in surprise.

'I say, you're a bit tiddly, I believe. You'd better not have any more beer.'

54

'What—is—*tiddly*?'

'I mean I think you're stinko, in fact a bit full.'

'Oh no! No! NO! Not this word again.' Maria collapsed in a chair, giggling. 'Not STINKING.'

'Shh, Maria! For Pete's sake—'

'I do not know Pete; I do not care for this Pete. I like to be tidd-ly. *Viva la musicá! Viva la birra!*'

She was now shouting, and several of the feminine guests were looking at her askance. Mitch went over to the piano to get Mandy's help.

Mandy came at once, but Maria had meanwhile found another full glass of beer on a table beside her, and was rapidly putting it away.

'Maria, don't drink any more beer. It's stronger than you think, and you've had enough—*basta, basta!*'

'I say, there's no need to swear at her,' protested Mitch. 'She doesn't know—'

'I'm not swearing. "*Basta*" means enough. Maria, dear, I think you need some fresh air. Let's come out on the veranda, *si*? Please, Maria.'

Maria was feeling wonderful, and ready to agree to anything. '*Si, si, si*, the veranda.' She got up, giggling, and cannoned into several guests on her way out, with profuse *Scusimis* and *Pregos*.

Mitch mopped her brow in relief as they got her into a garden seat. Bob Jordan was now singing, while one of the men banged on the piano keys. He revolved gently, intoning:

> 'I'm a little wild bush-flower,
> I grow wilder hour by hour;
> Nobody wants to cul-ti-vate me;
> I'm as wild as wild can be . . .'

'She's going to have an awful headache in the morning,' said Mandy, looking at the flushed Maria.

'I've got one already. That was Richard who rang up. He's demanding that I go home at once. Of course, I said I wouldn't, and he's furious. I'll have to go down next week-end and try to pacify him . . . Let's go home now, shall we?'

Mandy looked through the lighted windows at the largely middle-aged crowd within, now looking as unreal as figures on a stage seen from the wings. There had been a responsive light in Bob Jordan's eye, but she didn't really care if she never saw him again. 'All right; let's go,' she said.

'Andiam'!' cried Maria.

CHAPTER EIGHT

There was a Door to which I found no Key.
There was a Veil past which I could not see:
Some little Talk awhile of ME and THEE
There seem'd—and then no more of THEE and
  ME.

Once more the sand was screaming beneath the wheels; once more Mitch was sitting in the River train, being carried across the hot orange and salmon-red sand-hills, among bluebush and old-man saltbush and desert oak, towards the green oasis of Vindura.

This time she was alone, but she was well entertained; for in the next carriage was a group of young soldiers on their way back to camp. At every stop they leapt out, ran for the nearest bar, and came back laden with brown bottles of beer. In a short time these began to fly out of the windows, empty, to join the glassy cemetery of Dead Marines that lined the track on each side.

Somebody began to sing in a lugubrious voice:

'A soldier told me before he died,
I don't know whether the bastard lied...'

Blushing but interested, Mitch listened to the chronicle of the soldier's amazing invention, and then to the unexpurgated love-life of Abdul the Bul-Bul Emir, and the sad fate of Joe the Night-Watchman, with twenty-four kids and a terrible wife, with the roared chorus:

'Dinki-di, dinki-di,
I hope you don't think I
Would tell you a lie...'

Then the singing stopped, and an argument began. With drunken seriousness a young voice proclaimed: 'Well, so we bloody well ought to be friends with the bloody Eyeties and the Jerries now I mean, Christ we're all mother's sons, aren't we? But when these bloody things start, you've got to bloody well be in...'

The adjectives were strewed indiscriminately, and evidently had no reference to the actual bloodiness of war. Mitch felt an old, wise, maternal tenderness for the noisy young men next door.

Maternal! Heavens, was she getting broody? And did that mean—? But no, the effect couldn't possibly show so quickly. Really, Richard was very

57

careless, and had assured her that the same precautions were still effective the second time . . . For a scientist, he was terribly impractical. What if she should have a baby before they even had a home! It was just as well she would be sleeping a hundred and fifty miles away from him for the next month or two.

It had been wonderful to be with him again but the visit had been marred by long arguments and by the presence of his family. How tactfully—and how obviously!—they had let the young people go to bed early. It had made Mitch feel obstinate. They lay awake talking for hours, and the effort of arguing vehemently in a whisper had made her head ache.

She had convinced him at last, and he seemed resigned to the fact that she had no intention of coming home at present. Meanwhile, he was to keep scanning the columns of houses to let, and she had promised to return as soon as he found a home. And when he had a free Saturday he was coming up to Vindura for the week-end; they would take the bridal suite at the Community Hotel, he vowed, and at least have a place of their own for one night, whatever it cost.

His mother was delighted to have her son to herself again, and was spoiling him badly, of course. Thank goodness, thought Mitch, that he was being well looked after; she didn't have to feel guilty about leaving him to fend for himself, and he would appreciate her all the more after a separation. He was not the kind to console himself with other girls. He wanted her or no one. Dear Richard! If only he could be here too!

The voices next door had become quieter. It was

very hot, and Mitch felt drowsy; her head nodded with the rocking of the train. Then a notice-board caught her closing eyes:

NOTICE. The introduction of grapes, grape-vines and cuttings into South Australia is prohibited.
PENALTY £100.

They must be near the border. There was the dark indigo line of ragged trees that marked the course of the river; it was not far to Vindura. She began collecting her things, the home-made cake in a cardboard box that her mother-in-law had given her, her gloves, once white, from behind the seat, her overnight bag from the rack. She felt a surge of excitement, different from her first arrival when all was unknown. Outside the windows the first green rows of vines became visible, then they were whirling past like the spokes of some great wheel. The desert was past; the green leaves spread a wide carpet of welcome for her return.

*   *   *

The first rack was already laden with currant grapes. Ton after ton of purple fruit, untreated in any way, was tipped out and spread on the wire-netting layers to be dried and concentrated by the sun into black wrinkled currants.

Mitch and Mandy, being among the least skilled of the pickers, were taken off grape-picking for a few days and sent to pick pears. First they had to pick up windfalls, putting them into sweat-boxes to be peeled, cut and dried. These were bruised, squashy, and unpleasant to handle. Then they picked as high as they could reach, and then had a day riding round on the cart to reach the topmost branches.

The two lads, Tom and Dick, and Young Alf also rode on the cart, while Fearful Fred (as they had now named him) drove. It was a hilarious business, for Peanut, becoming restive at the circular motion, kept starting off with a jerk so that they fell over the back; or he moved off and left them clinging to a tree.

The youths, who were so nondescript that it was difficult to tell them apart, became very gallant about helping the two girls aboard, leaping down to lift them to their feet, and handing them up over the wheel.

At each occasion Mitch would bow deeply and say: 'Thanks, Rosencrantz and worthy Guildenstern,' while Mandy would murmur: 'Thanks, Guildenstern and worthy Rosencrantz.'

'Do they think we're bloomin' Jews or sumpin'?' Tom was heard to mutter to Dick.

Once when Mandy tumbled off alone, she landed awkwardly and wrenched her ankle. It was swelling visibly when Mike Hannaford came up to the group standing round her.

'I wish you wouldn't go knocking yourself about,' he grumbled. 'I'm short enough of pickers as it is, with Joe and Streak only half here. H'm, let's look at it. Can you walk?'

'I—think so. Oh! No, I can't.'

'Then I'll carry you. You'd better come up to the tanks and bathe it. You others go on; and Fred, try not to kill any of them, will you?'

'I carnt 'elp it. It's the bloody 'orse,' said Fred

morosely.

Even if she could have walked, Mandy would not have admitted it. As it was, her ankle was really painful.

Mike bent down, swung her off the ground, and carried her unceremoniously over his shoulder, as lightly as if she had been a child.

'This is known as a fireman's lift,' he explained.

'Thank you. Do you often go about rescuing damsels in distress from fires?'

'Often. I even light the fires so as I'll get the chance to rescue them.'

'That's a dangerous business.'

'What is?'

'Playing with fire.'

'Exciting, though.'

Did his grip about her knees tighten a little? His voice was impersonal. He strode steadily up to the rainwater-tank and set her down in the matted couch-grass beside it. With a handy stake he knocked the tap round, and held a folded khaki handkerchief under the water. Mandy had slipped her shoe off and was gingerly moving her foot.

'It's swollen quite a bit already.' He was squatting on his heels before her, in the comfortable pose in which she had first seen him, his old hat pushed to the back of his head. He took her slender brown foot in one hand, and ran long, sensitive fingers over the painful lump, pressing gently. 'That hurt?'

'Ow! Yes.' She looked up, and found his strange, smoky brown eyes upon her face. A response to something unspoken stirred in her deepest feminine being. It was as if he had said aloud: 'I desire you.' The response was instant, biological,

61

and profound. She continued to gaze into his eyes as though mesmerised, until he wrapped the wet handkerchief round the ankle and stood up abruptly.

'I'll put you over there in the shade of the sheds till the cart comes back, and Fred can drive you home.'

He picked her up again, but this time he held her cradled in his arms. It was only a few yards to the shade, but they were both intensely aware of every step. When he set her down again he was trembling slightly.

'Thank you. I'll let you have the handkerchief back,' said Mandy with her sweetest smile.

'That's all right. You'd better rest up tomorrow.' He went off to the racks without another look. Mandy was piqued and puzzled at his gruff tone, his abrupt departure.

*　　*　　*

Mitch was picking currants again, and because Fairy was away for the day as well as Mandy, she had Kurt Olmer for partner. The rapid click of his secateurs came through the vine, always a little ahead. He was picking through all the time, and since only the largest bunches on her side seemed to take his eye, her tins were filling very slowly with the small ones that he left.

'Goot crop just 'ere,' Kurt was saying amiably. 'Orfen, you find in ze middle of ze row like zis, ze fruit is all dried oop; but here he is goot all t'rough. No goot when ze bunches dry; craikey it's crook picken zen.'

'Must be crook,' said Mitch. She was getting a

little tired of cleaning up all the small bunches. She made a spurt, left a few behind, and reached through for a fat, shapely bunch on Kurt's side of the wire. Even as she grasped it the cutters flashed out and the bunch disappeared from view.

Kurt's face, square and smiling, appeared in a leafy aperture. 'Once more you take my bunches,' he said, smiling with square yellow teeth, 'and I snip the finger, so!' And he cut a thick vine-stem as though it had been butter.

Mitch stared at the slowly-oozing stump, and fell back quietly to her mopping-up operations. 'Craikey!' she muttered to herself.

Mandy and Fairy came back to work, in time for the great heat-wave at the beginning of March. For a week the temperature stood above 100 degrees. In the still, airless channels between the vines, the pickers could only guess at the temperatures they endured. Their guesses were extravagant, their comments on the weather profane.

Fred and Young Alf, riding about on the cart, created their own breeze and looked aggravatingly cool. They carried a water-bag of canvas slung underneath the cart, whose contents, cooled by evaporation, were in great demand among the pickers. Fred's shoulders had burnt to almost black, Joe's to a coppery brown with large freckles.

On the day when the thermometer reached 115 degrees in the shade, they knocked off early. Walton's sent down half a dozen bottles of cold beer, and they drank it in the shade of the vines. Maria was a little nervous of it—she had suffered a hang-over the day after the party—but she agreed after the first sip that there was nothing so thirst-quenching and satisfactory to a parched and dusty throat.

Fred insisted in giving a share to Peanut, though it worked out at only about a glass each. There were protests from all sides:

'Hey, what about us?'

'Don't waste it, Freddo!'

'Craikey, you give zat goodt beer to ze horse?'

'Peanut,' said Fred, ' 'as worked as 'ard as any of yz. Look 'ow 'e laps it up.'

For Peanut, with a look of bliss in his brown velvet eye, was sucking the last drop from the tin Fred had given him.

It was so hot the next day that Mitch and Mandy decided that they could not wait till after work for a swim. The main ditch on the block was still flowing, so as soon as they had eaten their lunch they made their way to a secluded part in the far corner of the block, shielded by a row of apricot trees.

Mother Mac and Maria went with them to 'keep nit', as they had no bathing-costumes with them, and Fairy decided to come too. Daisybud they did not ask; since the two lads had transferred their sidelong looks and audible remarks to the other girls, she had become politely remote. She was evidently used to being the belle of the block, and her nose was out of joint.

David took off his clothes and danced in and out of the water, looking like Tom the water-baby and bubbling over with questions and exclamations.

'Look at me, Mandy! Look at me, Maria! I can swim,' he shouted, lying on the bottom of the cement ditch and letting the shallow water flow over him as he kicked his legs. 'Look at me swimmin', Mum! Look at me swimmin', Mitch! C'n yous all swim as well as me?'

Mitch and Mandy took off all their clothes to feel the cool flow of water over their skins, but Fairy sat modestly encased in a pink shimmy and a huge pair of bloomers. Maria took off her shoes and paddled, while Mother Mac sat on the edge with her white, veined legs in the water.

'Look out!' she cried suddenly. 'There's a man having an eyeful. Up there by the sheds on the next block.'

'What! A Peeping Tom? I'll shame him,' said Mitch. She stood on the edge of the ditch, drew herself up, and pointed an accusing finger at the man. He had probably expected screams and a coy rush for clothes; now he slunk away behind the sheds, and was seen no more.

'I don't see why I should only have the water after youse girls,' complained Fairy. She got up, walked to a high point, and plumped down in the ditch. At once the water stopped flowing, except for a little trickle on each side of her; Fairy acted as a human dam.

'Did you hear,' said Mitch thoughtfully, 'about the cod that got into the irrigation channel once? It grew to be about a twenty-pounder.'

'Yes; they've got great big teeth on them like bulldogs, I believe,' said Mandy.

'Yes... Wouldn't it be funny,' said Mitch, 'if a big cod was to come up behind Fairy now, and bite her—well, you know where?'

They were all facing down-stream, Fairy at the back, David farthest in front. With a flick of her wrist Mitch sent a pointy piece of broken wood over their heads so that it fell in the channel behind Fairy. In a moment there was a scream; Fairy struggled to unwedge herself and stood up. 'I've been bit! Something bit me!' she yelled. The piece of wood was carried away past the others as the water was released with a rush.

'Probably only a tiger snake,' said Mandy soothingly. 'They get in the channels sometimes, too.'

'Oh! Ooh! I'm getting out.'

'Look at me swimmin'! C'n you see me swimmin', everybody?'

'I wish I had come in too. It is what you call very stink-ing hot.'

'Come on, Maria! Why don't you?'

'No time, girls. The whistle goes in a minute,' said Mother Mac.

They dressed, but saturated their shirts in the stream and put them on wet through. Mother Mac was horrified. 'You'll both get your deather cold!' she wailed. But the hot wind dried them five minutes after they were back at work. 'Oh for a swim in the dam!' they groaned.

They had taught Maria to dog-paddle about the dam, which was not very deep, and she had mastered the breast-stroke and was beginning to learn the over-arm stroke from Mandy, who was an expert instructress. On Saturday she was going to have her first swim in the river, for they had all been asked to a swimming party at the Riverside Club by moonlight.

Refreshed now by their channel dip, they began on a new row with enthusiasm, only to find that it was a mass of shrivelled bunches which fell to pieces at a touch. They seemed to have been attacked by a mildew which had since dried out, leaving a white web-like deposit.

Mrs Wilkes had told them that grapes were

sometimes attacked by odium, or downy mildew, and that they should not be picked with the others or they would contaminate the rest. So they began leaving behind and throwing away.

Their tins did not fill very fast, but they were making wonderfully swift progress up the row. They tossed bunches away with abandon, and ignored small ones altogether.

Suddenly Mandy noticed the lean figure of Mike Hannaford coming up the row behind her. He was bending to look into the vines, stooping to pick up a discarded bunch. She felt a ridiculous sense of guilt. Her heart began a foolish thumping.

He paused beside her. 'You're leaving a lot behind,' he said, without a smile.

'Oh yes, but it's no good, all mildewy. Mrs Wilkes said—didn't she, Mitch?—' she appealed through the vine, 'that it was better to leave it than contaminate the rest.'

'What you're throwing away isn't all bad by any means,' he said coldly. 'You'd better go back and pick up the biggest bunches. And clean up what's on the vine.'

'Yes, sir!' She felt that he was the boss, and she liked it. She had been spoiled and deferred to and adored so much that she found his terseness refreshing.

'Also, I hear that some of the pickers were swimming in the channel at lunch-time—without clothes. Chap on the next block complained.'

'Oh!' Mandy blushed slightly.

'Yes . . . Some blokes are hard to please.' He flashed her his sudden, disarming smile, and she felt her bones melt.

'I'm in love,' she thought, with a shock of joy, as

she turned back along the row. 'What, again?' said a little cynical voice at the back of her mind, but she ignored it.

The pattern of leafy light and shade on the ground reminded her of something... She remembered now: she had been quite young, about five years old, and she had been kept in for some naughtiness in the morning. The voices of the other children drifted in the open window, and a pattern of sunlight fell on her book. Beside her, not speaking, stood the adored kindergarten teacher, and in her heart was this flood of peace and joy...

'That must have been the first time I was ever in love,' she said to herself, picking up a crushed and dirty bunch.

As they were walking down to the dam that evening, the observant Mitch remarked: 'I notice that when Mike Hannaford has something to tell us, he always comes down your side of the row.'

'Does he?' said Mandy, with elaborate surprise.

'Oh, he is so nice!' exclaimed Maria. 'I have found he is a Roman Catholic, like me. I saw him at Mass on Sunday.'

Mandy looked at her with new attentiveness.

CHAPTER NINE

While the Rose blows along the River Brink,
With old Khayyám the Ruby Vintage drink:
And when the Angel with his darker Draught
Draws up to thee—take that, and do not shrink.

A hot north wind was blowing dust and sand about

68

the vineyard. The sky was white-hot, covered with a film of streaky cloud, and the air was taut with the electricity of pent-up storms.

Mandy screwed up her eyes against the unpleasant glare, feeling the dry wind burn her skin. The leaves of the currant-vines were blown inside-out, so that their papery undersides showed, and gave no impression of cool green. 'A real b— of a day,' said Mitch from the other side of the vine.

'It's giving me the most aw— aw— at-CHOO! awful hay-fever,' said Mandy, mopping her streaming eyes. 'Oh hell! I'd better take another anti-histamine, even if it does make me dopey. I'm going down to the tank for a drink.'

With her hair blowing into her eyes, a handkerchief to her swollen nose, she went before the wind. At the end of the row, with the tank in sight, she paused. Mike was converging upon it also, a kerosene-tin bucket in his hand. Don't be ridiculous, she said to herself sternly. What if he does see you like this? She went firmly on, and arrived just after him. He knocked the tap on for her and she filled her tin mug.

'What's up? Hay-fever? D'you get it from the currants?' he asked sympathetically.

'Yes, I've already taken a pill, but it's—a-rchoo! a-chah! worse than usual today. The north wind—'

'Ever tried a damp mask? Let me show you ...'

He took out another of his clean khaki handkerchiefs, wetted it beneath the tap, and wrung it out.

'Oh, but I haven't returned your other handkerchief yet. I was waiting for a chance to iron it.'

'Don't bother. Regard it as a gift,' he grinned.

'Now, turn around!'

She turned obediently, and felt the clammy, folded handkerchief slipped over her nose and mouth. He tied the corners in a knot at the back. A strand of her fine hair was caught in the knot; he released it with a gentle tug. Her heart began an uneven dance beneath her ribs.

He put both hands on her shoulders to turn her round again. 'God, you look like an Eastern princess now—most seductive.'

'But my hair is fair—'

'Golden. A princess in a fairy-story always has golden hair.'

'And I am not a princess.'

'You are to me. Beautiful—and unattainable.'

'In the fairy-stories I have read, the princess is never unattainable. She is won by some brave or remarkable action, like killing a giant or a dragon.'

'Unfortunately, there is a shortage of both those items in Vindura. Tell me what I can do.'

'Well, we have a near-witch up at Jordan's—Rosie Binks. Supposing you come up to tea at the cottage one Saturday—that is the only night she doesn't poison us with her witch's cooking.'

'This Saturday?'

'Well, we're going to a swimming party this Saturday, at the Riverside Club. Shall I see you there?'

'You will not. A mere foreman does not pollute the sacred precincts of the Riverside Club with his presence. Surely you've learnt by now how class-conscious the dear people of Vindura are? You must be the first picker ever admitted—it's unheard of. But the river is free. I might just be swimming about there somewhere.'

'Good. *Arrivederci*, as Maria says.'

'She's a nice kid.'

'Isn't she? Naïve, but very sweet.'

'Very.' They spoke absent-mindedly, looking into each other's eyes, not thinking of Maria at all. He broke the spell by bending to pick up his empty tin. Mandy made her way bemusedly back to her row.

In the afternoon David came running up to them, slipping in the loose furrows, clutching his little cotton sou'-wester against the wind. 'Mitch! Mandy!' he squeaked. 'Mike killed a 'nake. It was a big black one. Its head is all bloody. It nearly bited Maria.'

'Is she all right?'

'Yes, it didn't bit her, it only nearly did, and Mike killed it with a big 'tick—'

'Poor thing!' said Mitch. 'People are always killing snakes, but they have to live too. They won't hurt you if you leave them alone.'

'Oh Mitch! You'd be sorry for dingoes because they were so hungry they had to kill sheep. Wouldn't you kill a poisonous spider, for instance, if it was in the house?'

'Ye-es, I suppose. And I don't like centipedes, I admit.'

'I don't like 'nakes,' said David. 'They've got big teef, and they bite peoples.'

That night Maria told them, on the way home in the cart, what had happened. She had gone over to the small ditch at the end of her row, where there was still some water lying, to bathe her hot feet. A black snake had been cooling itself there in the wet mud.

71

It had risen menacingly hissing at her. Maria was so petrified that she could not run. Fortunately Mike had heard her screams; and, while Mother Mac clung on to David and stopped him from going any nearer, Mike broke its back with a stick and then battered it to death.

'Oh, he is so brave!' breathed Maria. 'There is this terrible serpent, *capite*, and I unable to move . . . He has saved my life.'

There was such a note of hero-worship in her voice that the others looked at each other significantly. Mandy said drily:

'He's lived on the river since he was a boy. Probably killed hundreds before now.'

She was thinking: 'It should have been me that he saved from the giant, the dragon, or the snake . . .'

Soon after eight on the following Saturday night they changed in the little dressing-shed belonging to the Club, and climbed down the steep bank to join the group of wet bathers on a raft moored among the willows.

There was much the same crowd as at the Jordans', and a few younger people. Beer and sandwiches were spread over the raft and the two dinghies moored alongside it. If it had not been for the mosquitoes it would have been perfect. Everyone was smoking to keep them at bay.

Mitch looked around her with delight. She had not known the river could be like this; it had seemed rather tame with its boats and willows by daylight, but now it spread broad and mysterious beneath the moon.

The trees on the far bank were black against the misty, light-charged air. Under a moon not quite at

72

the full, high in the eastern sky, the river sparkled with liquid light. Wild duck and waterhen, uttering their strange cries among the reeds, could be heard far over the still water.

Mandy, standing on the edge of the raft in her white costume preparing to dive, looked like a marble statue with bronze arms and legs. She went in cleanly, scarcely breaking the reflection of the moon.

Maria looked nervously at the great still flood of water. She sat on the edge and trailed her legs in the river, finding it surprisingly warm; but she had no wish to leave the raft and trust herself to those immense and unknown depths. Dog-paddling about the dam in sunlight was quite a different thing.

Mitch was not as good a swimmer as Mandy, and she felt a little qualm as she struck out alone into the middle of the stream, beginning to feel the gentle tug of the current. But the slight prickle of fear added to her enjoyment. She swam slowly, feeling the ends of her hair spread out in the water. The river was less buoyant than the sea, but was softer in its silken caress along her limbs. She swam into the path of the moon, and then turned on her back and floated, staring at its faintly distorted face.

Such a pure and liquid light was reflected from those barren moon-craters where there was no water, not even a drop of dew! 'Now I am one with the night,' she thought; 'I am the moon, and the flowing river, and the dark fish that glides among the rock-holes . . .'

But with that thought came a picture of the dim depths below, of the great cod nosing the weed, the transparent shrimps swarming in the mud, fifty, sixty, perhaps seventy feet down, where they waited to pick the bones of drowned creatures. She dropped her feet to tread water, and they went through the warmed surface water into the cold layer beneath. Immediately she began to panic. What if she got cramp?

She had drifted unconsciously with the current, and now the raft, the light-hearted group upon it marked by glowing cigarette-ends, seemed very far away. Would any of them notice if she failed to come back? Not for some time, probably. She felt suddenly overwhelmed with loneliness, and longing for Richard. Why wasn't he here? He was probably looking at this moon, and thinking of her.

Richard! She must get back safely for his sake, for the sake of the child they would one day have. She began to swim wildly, too fast, and was soon out of breath. The immense silent river, the enormous empty sky where the brilliant light of the moon had drowned the stars, seemed to press her down. She opened her mouth to cry out, and it filled with water. The current that had seemed imperceptible when she swam with it, was now too strong for her floundering progress. She must swim straight to the bank and hold on to a willow tree, though the thought of submerged boughs wrapping about her legs made her stomach go cold. She began to pray: 'Oh God, let Mandy notice. Oh God, let someone come . . .' The cold water was gripping her ankles, drawing her down.

'All right, turn over on your back and float. Don't panic.'

She turned with a gasping sob and flung her arms round the neck of her rescuer. Another human being seemed to her then the most wonderful miracle of the universe.

'Don't *clutch* me, or we'll both go under. Do as I say: turn over and float. I've got you.'

It was Mike Hannaford; how he happened to be there at that moment she had no idea. It was enough that he was there, that he was supporting her head in strong hands and drawing her rapidly through the water as he swam on his back with vigorous kicks.

By the time they reached the raft she was feeling rather foolish. She should not have gone so far alone, she should not have swum with the current to begin with, she should not have panicked when she knew perfectly well how to float.

Maria helped her up with cries and exclamations. 'Oh, *mamma mia* Mitch, what is it you have been doing? Oh, Mike, is she drowned? Are you all right, *mia povera*?'

Mitch collapsed on the edge of the raft, shivering, retching, and weeping a little with reaction from her fright. 'She'll be all right,' said Mike, holding on to a rope. Several hands reached down to pull him on board, he was slapped on the back and congratulated by the men, while the women gathered about Mitch in a clucking group.

Mandy came swimming back from up-stream, where she had gone some distance in the hope of coming across Mike. Now she found him established on the raft, with Mitch thanking him for saving her life. She felt unreasonably irritated at this second act of gallantry in which she was not involved.

'You certainly seem to make a habit of rescuing damsels in distress,' she said. 'However, I suspect

Mitch was quite capable of getting back by herself. She's been able to swim since she was ten.'

'I had cramp,' said Mitch indignantly and not quite truthfully. 'If it hadn't been for Mike—' she shuddered.

'You're chilled, and should get home to bed,' said Mrs Jordan. 'We've had our swim, and were going early anyway, we'll take you back to the cottage, won't we, Bob? Bob!' she said loudly. Bob Jordan wrenched his eyes away from Mandy's moonlit figure.

'Eh? Yes, certainly, we can take the girls home.'

'You stay, Miss Weston, since you're such a good swimmer, you won't want to come yet. Miss Delcalmo will look after this poor girl, won't you dear?'

'*Si, si!* I put her to bed, wrap her up warm. *Andiamo*, Mitch.'

'Sure you'll be all right, Mitch?' said Mandy perfunctorily.

'Yes, I'm all right now, really. But Mike deserves a medal.'

'Have a beer instead,' said one of the men, handing a full glass to Mike. 'Lucky you were about.'

'He is so brave! He has saved my life also,' said Maria, with worshipping eyes.

'Aw, come off it,' Mike grinned, embarrassed. 'Break it down, Maria.'

'I do not know what I am supposed to come off or break down; but I know you break the back of the serpent which has attacked me.'

'Better pipe down, mate,' said the man who had proffered the beer. 'You're a hero, and that's flat!'

Mitch was helped up the bank and into her

76

clothes, and Mandy returned to the raft. Someone was hospitably offering Mike a sandwich. He refused politely; emptied his glass; and with a 'So long, thanks for the beer,' dived neatly overboard.

Mandy was speechless. Here he was, by the greatest good luck, invited to join the party on the raft; here was she providentially freed of the company of Mitch, Maria, and the Jordans; and he just went off like that, without a word!

Someone called to her to bring her glass over to be filled, but she scarcely heard. She made a long, racing dive into the river and came up swimming. She could see the feather of foam from his thrashing legs just ahead as he drew away with a rapid crawl stroke towards the wharf. She put her head down and fairly tore through the water.

Fortunately he slowed up and began a leisurely side-stroke as he neared the wharf. She took a deep breath, dived, and came up from below, catching him by one ankle.

'Help! I thought a bunyip had got me.' She saw the white flash of his teeth in the moonlight, but she was still seething.

'Why did you go off like that?'

'Well, I couldn't very well stay on the raft. I don't belong with that mob.'

'What nonsense! They invited you aboard.'

'Yair—that was just charity. They were waiting for me to go.'

'Good Lord! You have got a chip on your shoulder, haven't you? Why didn't you stop and speak to me?'

'Aw, I dunno . . . I thought—'

'You thought I was just a snob, too? Oh, Mike! You're a nicer bloke than all "that mob" put

77

together. Come on—race you to the steps.'

Her anger had evaporated. She suddenly felt tremendously happy, for she had remembered that the only reason Mike was here, the only reason he could have been swimming about in the vicinity of the raft when Mitch got into difficulties, was that she had told him she would be here tonight.

He reached the wharf steps just ahead of her, and turned to give her a hand and help her up. She emerged dripping and gleaming in the moonlight in her white costume that fitted like a skin. He drew in his breath with a just audible gasp as he looked at her.

They sat on the edge of the wharf, where the wood was still warm from its daylong soaking in sunshine, and dangled their legs above the water, while their chests heaved with the exertion of their fast swim.

'You certainly move through the water,' she said.

'You're not bad yourself.'

She pulled off her helmet-like white cap and ran her fingers through her short fair hair, looking at him provocatively, her head a little on one side.

'What are your plans for this evening, Mr Hannaford? I'm on my own.'

'Well, I have a car here—parked up by the Post Office. But—your friends—'

'They've gone home. I'll have to slip back to the raft, and say good-bye, and get dressed. See you up there in half an hour.'

She would think of some excuse for leaving the swimming party, discourage any of the men who offered to accompany her, and make her way to the Post Office. She could say she had to make a trunk

78

call to the city. As she swam back to the raft she thought that all the water in this great river could not quench the fire burning in her heart.

CHAPTER TEN

One Moment in Annihilation's Waste,
One Moment, of the Well of Life to taste—
The Stars are setting and the Caravan
Starts for the Dawn of Nothing—Oh, make haste!

'Have you ever been out to the Lock?' Mike turned with his arm resting on the steering-wheel.

'No, but I'd like to see it.' It had taken her some time to extricate herself from the swimming party and to change into her slacks and white cotton jumper and get up to the Post Office, and she had been afraid he would think she was not coming. But he was still waiting in his car, a big sedan of a rather old model.

Her costume was rolled up in her towel. She dumped it on the back seat and felt her hair with both hands. 'My hair got wet after all. Does it look terrible?'

'I can't see it. I can only see the brightness of your eyes.' With perfect naturalness he put up a hand and felt the damp strands. 'It *is* wet. Sure you won't catch cold?' For she had shivered slightly at his touch.

'No! Come on, let's go. *Andiamo!*'

He started the car, and soon they were bumping along the winding road to the Lock. They talked of mutual acquaintances. Mandy found that Mike

79

didn't like Mr Pike or Bob Jordan any more than Mitch did.

'The land means nothing to them,' he said. 'It's just something to exploit, to get as much money out of as possible per acre. This place, the way it's been built up in the desert, the seasonal cycle in the vineyard—it *means* something to me, though I don't own even a quarter of an acre of it.'

'And it doesn't to Mr Jordan?'

'Still less to Walton, who sits on his tail in the city and rakes in the profits. Do you suppose he's ever planted a vine-cutting, or sweated over a dip? It's all just profits to him.'

'A vineyard by the river's brim
A prosperous vineyard was to him,
And it was nothing more,'

she misquoted.

'Eh? Yes, that's about it. I've got a theory that the people who work the land ought to own it, or at least share in it. I'm saving up to get my own block anyway.'

'Good for you.'

She could hear the roar of the water over the weir before they reached the Lock. It had a sound of doom about it. They got out, and he steadied her across the narrow top of the Lock-gates to the wider cat-walk above the weir.

The moon was now overhead. The river above the weir lay in a great still pool, reflecting the sky's light. The water fell six feet over the weir to the level below with a ponderous roar, and broke into a sparkling mass of white foam.

Mandy leant on the guard-rail, fascinated, and

watched the mighty weight of water sliding beneath her feet. Quite near the weir it appeared not to move; then it suddenly speeded up, seemed to gather itself together, and fling itself over the edge in a curving wall of glass.

'Like someone who sees that death is the only way out,' she murmured, 'and, without waiting to be carried by circumstance, flings himself to destruction.'

'What are you muttering about? Death? On a night like this?' and he swept his arm to include the moon-sparkling water, the dark trees, and the vast purity of the sky. 'All the same,' he said soberly, 'there'd not be much hope for anyone who fell in there. I've seen a log caught for days in the whirlpool, rising and turning and being swamped over and over again.'

She was silent. The doom-like roar of the water had brought some lines into her head, and she was trying to recall them . . . Ah! yes:

'What was I? What was I? Nothing
But a Moment, aware
of the ruins of Time.'

Mandy had withdrawn into an unexpected mood of melancholy; she was given to these sudden ups and downs. She wished he would take her in his arms and kiss her into forgetfulness, yet she felt too depressed and inert to make the first move.

Meanwhile, he waited in unbearable tension for some sign from her. He had never met anyone quite like Mandy before, and he did not know what to make of her. She seemed unconventional, yet she had a proud, aloof profile, and she was—God help him!—a 'lady'. The very accents of her voice paralysed him.

'Shall we—' He cleared his throat nervously, and shouted over the roar of the water; 'Shall we go back now?'

'All right. If you like,' she said indifferently.

They made their way back to the car in silence. He looked at her anxiously before he started the motor. Was she offended for some reason?

'Is anything wrong?' he said. 'You seem ... sad.'

She stared out at the river, her head averted. 'I just had a tremendous impulse to throw myself over there, that's all.'

'How strange you are!'

'No, not really. My mother took her own life, when I was still a child,' she said abruptly. 'I still don't know why ... But sometimes I feel that I must go the same way.'

'You mustn't say that. You're young, and healthy, and your life, almost the whole of life, is in front of you. Do you often feel like this?'

'Not often.' She turned with a pale smile. 'Let's go now.'

They parted outside the Jordans' block, the air between them still thick with words unspoken and caresses ungiven.

As he drove violently back to the town, Mike was cursing himself for missing such an opportunity; yet he could not have risked the blow to his self-esteem if she should snub him. He wanted her more than ever.

*   *   *

The currants were nearly finished. When there was only one row left, all the pickers descended on it and worked like mad to fill their last tins, until the vines heaved and billowed like a green sea.

Maria was anxious to fill her tin. She wanted to show Mike, by her good tally, that she really was learning to be a good picker; once they started on the unfamiliar sultanas her tallies would drop again. And she needed the money. She was saving to buy a new, pretty dress to wear to Mass on Sunday, when she hoped to see Mike. She had nearly enough to get it this coming Saturday.

Daisybud was coming towards her from the opposite direction, picking like a machine. They both reached for the last fat bunch together. Daisybud removed it neatly and fell back, panting. The currants were finished. A cheer went up from the pickers.

'Here, you better have this; my tin's full,' said Daisybud generously. 'Better top your last one up a bit,' and she began removing bunches from her own last tin into Maria's.

This generosity from her rival of a few minutes ago warmed Maria.

'What will we do now?' she asked, smiling at Daisybud whose usually immaculate waves were disarranged.

'Shaking down, most likely.' She pulled out a small pocket-mirror.

'You mean—?'

'Shaking down currants from the racks. You'll get your arms nearly pulled out of y'r shoulders.' Daisybud licked one finger, and passed it over the thin line of her eyebrows.

Down at the racks, the pickers sat about yarning

or leaned on posts. The serious business of getting in the currant crop was over; there had been no rain to split the fruit, and much of it was already dry.

At a word from Mike Hannaford they lined up on each side of the racks that had been spread early. Taking each wire-netting layer in turn as he loosened it, they bounced it up and down between them.

The dry, brittle bunches fell to pieces. Currants shot off stems, rained to the hessian at the bottom, flew through the air, and went down necks and inside shoes. A false sole of squashed currants formed on their shoes; Mother Mac accused Mrs Wilkes of treading on as many as possible so that she could scrape them off at home and make a currant cake.

It was great fun, and young Davey ran about between people's legs, getting in the way and squealing with delight. It was raining currants; he had never seen so many before.

In the afternoon they began upon the sultanas, and now everyone had to use a knife. The bunches were irritatingly brittle; at the slightest touch the twigs broke and the berries fell like hail. Yet the main stem was tough, far too tough to be broken by hand, and it was often twisted about the central wire of the trellis. Maria, almost in despair, found herself hacking at the wire instead of the stem, blunting her knife and getting nowhere. She saw the pretty dress fading farther away.

'You want to take it slow at first, love, till you get the knack,' said Mother Mac kindly.

Nack! thought Maria irritably. Nack, neck, knock, nick, they all sounded the same, yet some had a K in front and some didn't, and what in the

84

name of all the saints was a nack, anyway? What a
horrible language! And she was tired of asking
questions, and being treated like a child, a silly
bambina.

The real reason for her ill-humour was that Mike
had asked the other two girls, Mandy and Mitch, to
come down to the racks and help with spreading the
dipped sultanas. Not that she wanted to be put on
to spreading herself; she could make more money
on piecework and she preferred to work among the
vines. But Mike was working at the dip, which
meant that he would be close to Mandy all day.
Maria's dark eyes had noted the way Mike looked
at the beautiful blonde one. Yet it was she, Maria,
who had been rescued by him from the serpent . . .

Ever since she had found that he had the same
religion, she had nursed a wild dream about Mike
Hannaford. He was taller than Mario, and not so
sturdy, yet he had the same thick, dark hair and
golden-brown eyes . . . Yet, he reminded her of
her lost Mario. If only, one day, he might take his
place!

Down at the racks, Mitch and Mandy worked in
large rubber gloves, moving the piles of glistening
bunches as they were tipped on to the wire. They
had to be spread evenly in a single layer, and
because of their fragility they must be moved with
the utmost care, with a gentle rolling motion.

The sultanas were more amber-coloured than
green, ripened to perfect sweetness by the inland
sun, swollen to juicy fullness by water from the
river. Peanut loved them in any state; he would pull
a bunch from the vine and crunch it with its leaves,
while juice ran down his hairy chin; he would take a
wet mouthful from the rack and eat it, caustic,

potash and all; and once he browsed right through a loaded tin waiting to be dipped, until driven off with blasphemous cries.

'It's a bloody wonder that 'orse doesn't bust,' said Fred admiringly.

The two lads, Tom and Dick, had also been taken from the picking ranks to propel the little trolley loaded with dipped fruit along the line from the dip to the rack. They seemed a bit overawed by Mandy's cool beauty, but Tom began paying attentions to Mitch.

'Eh, what about comin' into the dance Saturdee night?' he muttered in her ear in passing.

'Thanks, worthy Rosencrantz, but my husband wouldn't like it.'

'Garn, you're not married! And me name's Tom; not Rosen-whatsit.'

'Mandy, he doesn't believe I'm a married woman.'

'Show him your ring.'

Mitch pulled off a wet rubber glove and displayed the small silvery band on her left hand.

'Get a load of that, Dick,' said Tom wonderingly. 'She is married!'

'And my husband is coming up to Vindura next week, and he's a crack shot.'

Tom faded away towards the dip.

The dip was worked by a large, brawny, rugged-faced, jovial and blasphemous person called Merv. He had a nose like the backbone of a mountain range, and teeth like marble tombstones. He worked with unfailing good-humour in the heat and steam of the dip, like a jolly devil supervising the boiling pitch in Hell. The dip-tins had handles, and holes punched through them to let the liquid

86

out again as he passed each one through the dip with the same steady, unhurried motion.

*   *   *

Mandy felt that she knew Mike Hannaford ever so much better since their drive out to the Lock, even though she was puzzled by his restraint on that occasion.

So when she saw him close beside her scowling at the spread sultanas and muttering to himself, she said cheerfully: 'What's up Mike? Are we butchering them?'

'Not you; it's that idiot Merv. He's got too much caustic in the dip. See these great cracks in the skins? Absolute mincemeat! They'll dry out too quick and turn dark, and dark fruit means a lower grade. Not that they're any different, mind you; but women seem to like pale golden fruit the best. That's why you have to be so careful in spreading, not to make berries. The berries fall to the bottom and turn dark.'

Mandy smiled. 'I like you to lecture me on the properties of dried fruits.'

'Was I lecturing? I suppose I was. You're not really interested, are you?'

'I like to listen to *you*. I wouldn't if it were Bob Jordan talking.'

He gave her a long, intimate look before he went off to complain to Merv. Mandy, warmed and elevated—hadn't he brought her to work at the racks so that they should be near each other?—heard the beginning of Merv's luridly-embroidered reply before it was lost in the rattle of the returning trolley:

87

'But just now I topped it up with water, and it was too bloody weak, so I puts some more flamin' caustic...'

CHAPTER ELEVEN

Indeed, indeed, Repentance oft before
I swore—but was I sober when I swore?
And then—and then came Spring, and Rose-in-hand
My threadbare Penitence apieces tore.

An empty wine-bottle came whizzing out of the back door of the Binks's cottage and stopped the girls in their tracks. It was lunch-time on Saturday, and they were all dressed in their best, ready for a visit to town. They were going to choose a new dress for Maria.

'Ha-ha-ho-HO-HO,' came from within like the laugh of a slightly crazy kookaburra. 'Missedyer, didden I? Whatsamatter withyer?'

They looked at each other questioningly. It was Rosie's voice, and Rosie was obviously rather the worse for wine.

'Come orf it, Rose. Yer mighta smashed a window.'

'Ah, go on. I coulda hityer if I tried.'

Mitch advanced, and cautiously put her head in the door. 'Lunch ready, Mrs Binks?' she asked cheerfully.

'Come on in, come on in, girls. Make yerselves at our place. Outa me way, Fred. Can'tyer see them girls is starvin'?'

She leered drunkenly at the girls and waddled

into the kitchen after the morose Fred. There were several crashes and curses before she came back, balancing three plates of cold meat and a bottle of tomato sauce.

'There, y'are, girls. Get that into yer.' She slammed the sauce-bottle down in the middle of the table. 'I got a bloomonge for th' next course, real pretty.'

When she went out the girls winked at each other silently.

'Under the weather,' muttered Mitch.

'Full as a boot,' said Mandy.

'You mean stink-o, *non è vero? Troppo del vino?*'

'Completely troppo,' said Mitch.

When Rosie came in with the 'bloomonge' they all fell silent, staring at the horrible amorphous mass that was visibly spreading its pseudopodia over a large flat plate, like an enormously-magnified, bright pink amœba.

'It never kept its shape,' Rosie was complaining. 'It looked real beaut in the mould before I tipped it out. It'll taste better than it looks, though.'

'It had better!' said Mitch.

There was silence again for a long half-minute while they waited for the storm to break. But Rosie's blood-shot eyes had lost their brooding fire. 'Try it an' see, anyways,' she said amiably.

Gingerly they helped themselves to small serves, while Rosie leant on the table, humming tunelessly. Mandy took one mouthful, and laid her spoon down decisively.

'It's uneatable. It's got no taste.'

'It tastes faintly pink, that's all.'

'*C'e orrible!*'

'Mrs Binks,' said Mitch, becoming more courageous as the lightning failed to strike, 'you cannot expect us to eat this concoction of gooey, gelatinous gobs masquerading as a pudding.'

'All right, don't eat it then!' Rosie swooped on the dish and flung it through the back door after the bottle. There was a crash as it hit the fig tree, and pieces of 'bloomonge' went flying through the air. Rosie laughed delightedly.

A high scream of outrage came from beyond the door; then Di-anne appeared, arrayed in white socks and shoes and an organdie dress. A large dollop of bright pink goo clung to her curls, which she clawed at frantically.

'OO! I'll tell my mummy on you, I will!' she shrilled.

The girls let out a simultaneous shriek of laughter; Fred poked his head round the kitchen door to see what was going on.

'I'll tell my mummy, so there!' sobbed Di-anne.

'Go on then; go and tell her!' cried Rosie, picking up the sauce-bottle as if she might let fly with that next. 'Always snooping around!'

Di-anne fled, shrieking. For the first time Mitch knew a fellow-feeling for Rosie.

'Good for you, Mrs Binks; she's a little horror.'

Fred ambled in with some bread and jam to take the place of the pink stuff; Rosie fetched a new bottle of wine and asked them to join her. Soon they found that in her alcohol-softened mood they could ask anything of Rosie. They told her they would rather have fresh fruit for dessert, and salads for their lunch, and it would mean less cooking for her. They would rather have half a cucumber or a tomato with bread and butter than the meat sandwiches flavoured with garlic that she was so fond of preparing; and would she mind cutting down on the very hot curry?

Rosie agreed to everything, except that she insisted they should still have meat breakfasts on working days: 'No one's going to say that Rosie Binks is mean with her boarders . . .'

They parted amicably, with Rosie promising to make them hot scones in the morning.

However, there were no scones for Sunday morning breakfast. They came home from town, very late, having missed the last bus after the pictures and walked home, carrying their shoes, along the bitumen road which felt firm and warm beneath their bare feet. There was still a light over at the other cottage. Sounds of drunken singing and the occasional smash of breaking crockery drifted through the clear, still night.

'They're having a real bender,' said Mitch, pausing to listen to a particularly loud crash.

'They are breaking things, more than just bending them, I think,' said Maria.

'Oh, Maria, I love you; you are so quaint and literal.'

'*Deh!* What have I said now?'

'Nothing, *cara mia*. Come in and try on the dress. You look stunning in it.'

'As long as I am not "stinking"!'

'You're very quiet tonight, Mandy. It's not like you to stand about staring at the stars. If I didn't know better I'd think you were in love.'

'Oh, shut up, Mitch!'

It was the middle of the morning before a surly shout from the cottage summoned them to breakfast. They went in quietly to find a plate of burnt toast, carelessly buttered, in the middle of the table. Rosie came in with a pot of tea, and they just managed not to gasp. Her mouth was cut and swollen, and one eye was blackened. The look in her remaining good eye was enough to keep them silent. She went out without a word.

They sat glumly crunching the incinerated bread. Maria was depressed because, though she had put on the new dress and gone to early Mass, Mike was not there. Mandy was abstracted, wondering how she could arrange to see him again away from other people; and Mitch was in a state of suppressed excitement because she was waiting for a trunk call to come to the house from Richard, confirming his visit next week-end.

They did their weekly wash and then sun-bathed for the rest of the morning. When Di-anne came over with the message that there was a trunk-line call from the city for Mrs Fairbrother, Mitch could almost have kissed the unpleasant child.

It was Richard, his own dear voice. Its tones had a physical effect on her, they vibrated in her nerves and made her weak with love. And he was coming on the plane next Saturday; he had already booked the bridal suite. Recklessly, Richard went on for another three minutes when the pips sounded. They couldn't afford it, but what did it matter? They couldn't afford the bridal suite, either.

Mitch hung up in a daze of happiness, and saw Mrs Jordan hovering at the end of the hallway where she had obviously been listening.

'My husband's coming up to join me for the week-end, isn't it wonderful?' she cried happily.

'Well, how nice for you!' smirked Mrs Jordan. 'It'll be a real second honeymoon, won't it?'

Mitch felt slightly ill. She hated that sickly word, honeymoon. Thank goodness she hadn't mentioned the bridal suite!

Mrs Jordan lowered her voice as though the walls might have ears. 'As for that disgusting couple over at the cottage, they're always fighting. Did you hear the goings on yesterday? Drunk, of course. The woman threw pink custard all over Di-anne.'

'I don't think she meant to. But they *had* been drinking wine. She looks sorry for herself this morning, poor old trout.'

'H'm! She'll be drinking again this afternoon. Once they start, it goes on the whole week-end.'

It was evident that Fred and Rosie had been sampling several hairs-of-the-dog by the afternoon. The three girls were just setting out for a walk when the jinker came tearing down the drive with Fred holding the reins, Rosie beside him, and a nearly full flagon of wine rolling about on the floor.

Rosie had regained her amiability of yesterday. She smiled in a friendly fashion from her battered face. Fred, too (although his seamed face was scored with long scratches from Rosie's thorn-like nails), gave one of his sinister grins. He pulled up with a jerk.

'Hop up, youse girls,' cried Rosie. 'We're goin' down to the river, for a pickernic. Want to come?'

They looked at each other, hesitating. The Binkses certainly looked a villainous pair in the afternoon sunlight. But the river . . .

'Come on!' said Mitch, and began climbing up the side of the cart. Mandy shrugged, and climbed after her. Maria, however, hung back. 'I have much mending to do. I think I will go a little walk, and then come back. I will be getting the tea for us,' she said.

'Gerrup, Peanut!' roared Fred, and almost running over Maria they went galloping out the gate, with a swirl of dust and a scattering of gravel. Whether Peanut had been sharing in the celebrations, or was just infected by his driver's recklessness, he tore along the red sandy road beside the railway-line, round the corner on two wheels and up the green willow-bordered lane beside the property like a mad thing.

Quite suddenly they passed the end of the last irrigated block; the lane opened out into flat grey saltbush country, dotted with clumps of old-man saltbush and bluebush, a few steel-blue box trees, and the dark shapes of desert oak. The vines were a green dream behind them; the landscape was now a symphony of blue and grey, with an indigo band of distant gum trees marking the course of the river ahead.

Rosie sang; the girls hung on tensely to the sides of the rattling, bouncing cart. A dry roly-poly bush blew across the track, and Peanut pretended to shy at it. They were too nervous to speak.

This was sheep country, though it looked like desert and they saw no sheep; it took a whole acre to feed one animal. Mitch hopped down to open the first gate, which bore the polite legend: 'PLEASE Shut The Gate.' Rosie opened the next, which said more tersely: 'SHUT THE GATE.' Mandy mumbled out of the cart, laughing, to open the last one before the river. It said in large white letters painted on a square of tin:

'SHUT THE BLOODY GATE.'

The track now wound in and out of the big trees, and down a slope of grey-white sand to the edge of the river. Mitch was out of the cart before it had stopped; and climbing out on a great red-gum root that projected over the water, sat staring at the river.

This, this was how she had expected it to be: sun-drenched, silent, grey-green, immense, not closed between walls of green willows as in the cosy town; not cold and glassy as it had been beneath the moon.

Farther down it broadened out into a lagoon, an overflow filled with the skeletons of grey, drowned trees. A smaller backwater was covered with a red film of floating duckweed, and beside it a white crane stood like an alabaster image on a fallen log.

Mitch drew in her breath with delight. Mandy was muttering something behind her about wishing she had brought her costume so that she could have a swim. Mitch scarcely heard her. She was staring across the river towards the up-stream bend, where a wisp of thin smoke was curling among the trees. The sky above was intensely blue.

There was quite a collection of huts there, she saw now—mere humpies built of hessian or of rusted kerosene tins beaten flat, and roofed with old bits of tin, sheets of bark, or branches of dead gum-leaves. Two or three women in bright dresses moved among them. Several dinghies were pulled up on the bank, and a dark-faced man was baiting a set-line for cod.

'What's that, Mrs Binks? It's almost like a little settlement out in the bush.'

'Yeah, that's the blacks' camp,' said Rosie. 'It's not so far out of town, the river bends around a lot.

95

But they have to keep on the far bank of the river; the council won't let them live on this side.'

'What, aborigines? Where?' said Mandy, interested.

'Over the river there.'

'You mean they have to live in those terrible dumps?'

'They're not allowed to build in the town, anyways. They haven't got much chance to live decent, even if they wanted to.'

'And once they owned the whole country,' said Mandy softly. 'The river belonged to them, and all the fish in it; the bush, and all its kangaroos. And now . . .'

'There's not many full-bloods left now, only half-castes and quarter-bloods; and *their* children you can't hardly tell the difference, like Mike Hannaford, f'rinstance,' said Fred. He stopped and blinked at the burning gaze that Mandy turned upon him.

'Like WHOM?'

'Like Mike, you know, the foreman at the other block. I'm just as dark as he is, to look at.'

Mandy continued to stare at him.

'Are you sure?' asked Mitch.

'Course I'm sure. Mike's gran'ma was born over the river, but it don't make no difference. Mike's as white a feller as you'll find anywhere. His old man fought in the last blue for Australia; and Mike would of been in it if 'e'd bin old enough. He's a good bloke, Mike; a real gentleman.'

'Yair, Mike's all right,' said Rosie.

Mandy wondered why she should be so struck by the simple fact of Mike's heredity. In the city, perhaps, it would have meant less; out here, in the country, where the miserable remnants of the once-flourishing Murray tribes lived as outcasts beyond the town, it seemed of immense moment. She could understand things about him that had puzzled her before. She stared musingly across the water at the collection of huts.

Alf hung a feed-bag over Peanut's nose, and he and Rosie disposed themselves among the arm-chair-like roots of a great tree. They seemed to have brought no other refreshments on the 'pickernic' than the flagon of sweet wine which passed between them regularly.

Mitch and Mandy looked at each other uneasily. Fred's driving had been erratic enough on the way out; how was he ever going to negotiate the gate-posts on the way home?

They took off their shoes and paddled in the shallow, lukewarm water at the edge.

'Ow! Yabbies!' cried Mitch as something nipped her toe. They hastily got out and, peering from the tree roots down into the milky-green water, saw the dark shapes of the small crayfish moving about, waving their feelers gently.

'If only we had some bait!'

They searched up and down the bank, and beside a stick which had evidently held a set line they found a rather dried-up fish's head. Fred produced some string from his pocket, and they were soon absorbed, Mandy fishing while Mitch made a landing-net from a piece of wire and some hessian found in the cart.

The silly, greedy crayfish, once they caught hold with their big claws, would not let go until they were drawn almost to the surface. Then Mandy slipped the net behind them, and as they shot off backwards towards the bottom they were caught.

Soon they had two dozen imprisoned in the cart, where they clambered over each other, blew bubbles, and waved their claws menacingly. Their backs were a beautiful iridescent blue.

'I wish we had a tin or a box to put them in,' said Mandy. 'I don't fancy travelling home with them clambering all over my feet. Not in *sandals*, I mean . . .'

'I don't fancy driving with Fred in the state he'll be in soon, for that matter,' said Mitch.

'Let's walk back, shall we? They can have the yabbies.'

'All right.'

They told the others that they had decided to explore along the river-banks a little way, and then cut back across country to the block.

Rosie, her head resting on Fred's khaki shirt-front, waved her hand amiably.

'Don't get lorst,' said Fred. 'Y' could do a perish away from the river.' But there was little chance of their getting lost with the river trees for a landmark, visible over the flat plains for miles.

CHAPTER TWELVE

Come, fill the Cup, and in the Fire of Spring
The Winter Garment of Repentance fling:
The Bird of Time has but a little way
To fly—and Lo! the Bird is on the Wing.

Maria had a great deal of ironing to do. Where the other girls had washed only a pair of blue jeans each and two or three shirts, she had washed three cotton dresses and five gathered aprons for she wore a clean one to work every day.

She wished she could wear the becoming new dress to work, since Mike had not been there to see it at church this morning. Mandy always managed to look lovely even in her old stained jeans; but Maria was secretly convinced that no man liked to see a girl in trousers.

She sighed, folding the last apron and putting it on the freshly-ironed pile. Who ironed Mike's shirts for him, she wondered, and sewed on his buttons, and mended his socks? Did he have a mother, or a sister? She knew that he did not have a wife. It was surprising that he was not married, such a handsome young man and with a good job; for surely every man wanted to marry and have some *bambini* of his own?

She was day-dreaming about a little boy with a brown face and white teeth like Mike's, when Mrs Jordan's voice fluted at her from the door of the laundry:

'Oh, Miss Delcalmo, you won't forget to fold the ironing-blanket, will you, dear? And see that the iron is unplugged. It was left plugged in last week.'

'*Si, si, si,*' said Maria, and pulled the iron-plug out of the wall. 'I am Missus Delcalmo,' she muttered rather sullenly, but Mrs Jordan had gone.

Maria walked back to the cottage with the coloured dresses and aprons folded in a pile almost to her chin. At the door she stopped. There was a car pulled up beside the back fence. As she hesitated, Mike Hannaford came round from the back door.

'Oh, there you are! I was beginning to think

there was no one home,' he said, smiling.

Maria blushed. 'There is no one home, only me.' Oh, why had she changed her dress before he came?

'So you've been ironing? How domesticated! Let me carry them in for you.'

'No, no, it is all right ... *prego* ... do not bother,' she said awkwardly.

He held the wire door open for her, and followed her in. Maria was dreadfully embarrassed. There was only the one room, except for the tiny kitchen, and the room was full of beds. She began putting her clothes away in the rickety chest-of-drawers.

'It was Mandy—Miss Weston—who asked me to come, actually,' said Mike, sensing her restraint. He did not seem depressed at Mandy's absence, however. '"Come up to tea on Saturday," she said. Something about rescuing her from the old witch who usually gets your meals—'

'Oh, that is Mrs Binks, the wife of Fred, you understand ... Mandy and Mitch have gone with them on a—a pickernik, I think she said, down by the river.'

'A picnic. And they didn't invite you?'

'They ask me, yes; but I have much ironing, I am busy, as you see. I am to get the tea ready before the others return.'

She went through to the lean-to kitchen and began clattering the few saucepans.

He came and lounged in the kitchen doorway, one hand on the lintel over his head. 'Gosh! I could scarcely stand up in there. What are you making for tea? Can I help?'

'Oh—omelettes, I am thinking. But perhaps you could light the kerosene stove for me? I am a little

100

nervous of it.'

'Well, you don't need to start yet.'

Maria looked confused. 'I thought perhaps a cup of tea? I cannot offer you wine.'

'That's all right. I've got beer in the car, and a bottle of gin, and lemon squash—the lot. Hold on, I'll get them. Never mind making tea.'

As soon as he'd gone Maria dashed to the mirror in the outer room and did her hair. She looked longingly at the new dress, hanging on the wall . . .

Fortunately Mike came in backwards, his arms full of bottles. As he edged past the swinging wire door, Maria gave a small scream.

'*Momento, signor—si vi piace*—I am not ready. I am changing my dress. Do not look, please!'

'All right, but hurry, before I drop these bottles—my sole contribution to the feast. I'll count a hundred.'

He began counting slowly, but then faster and faster, till he gabbled: 'Ninety-nine, hundred, coming-ready-or-not!'

He turned to see Maria, flushed and with her beautiful, abundant dark hair disarranged, doing up the demure white collar of a blue dress. It had a youthfully full skirt and became her very well.

Mike whistled. 'Some dress, Maria!'

'You mean it pleases you?'

'I'll say! Didn't the boys ever whistle at you in the street in Italy?'

'No . . . They do not whistle. Sometimes they made a hissing noise, sss-ss! or said *Bellezza*—that is "Beauty" in English.'

'I'll bet they did!'

Maria smoothed her hair. 'I didn't see you at Mass this morning, Mr—Mr Mike.'

101

'Just Mike will do. No, I'm a back-slider, I'm afraid. I must go next week, before Father O'Toole comes after me.'

'Do you go to Confession, M—Mike?'

'No; I'm not a very good Catholic, as I said. In Italy, I imagine, the Church is different, stronger ... a real part of the people's lives. Here, we live so much out-of-doors, and ... I don't know. Sometimes I feel nearer to God on a spring day in the vineyard, with the little leaves sprouting from the dead wood, than in that rather ugly modern church in the town.'

'Yes, it is different, I think. Our churches are so old. You open the door, or go past the leather curtain, and inside it is dark, and quiet, and peaceful, with only the candle-flames and the coloured windows to give light. There is a smell of ... I went once to the Public Library in Melbourne, and it had this smell, of something old, and precious ... The air is holy.'

'Yes, I understand.' He was staring at her meditatively, her pale Madonna-face and waving dark hair above the blue dress. Maria ... Santa Maria ...

'Then there are the feast days and the processions and the Festival of the Car at the *Duomo* in Firenze ... Religion is gay in Italy, sometimes.'

Florence, and Mario ... His image was faint as a ghost's.

Mike had put the bottles down on the table in the middle of the room. 'Well, let's be gay too. Any glasses?'

'Only cups. I will get some.'

She brought the thick white cups from the

kitchen, while Mike produced a bottle-opener. He opened the beer, but Maria shook her head. She said that she was frightened of Australian beer, she once had a very little and it went to her head.

'I would have thought it was safer than gin; however, I'll mix you a mild gin squash,' said Mike.

She thought it tasted like a plain fizzy drink, and finished it quickly. 'It was hot ironing, and I am thirsty,' she said, holding out her empty glass to be filled. Mike looked at her in some surprise, but mixed her another, and poured himself a second beer.

Maria's dark eyes were very bright. Through the cottage windows she could see the feathery rows of the vines, intensely green in the yellow light of afternoon. If only there were wine, and music, she would feel quite at home. Her knees felt rather weak, they were aching in a queer way. She sat down on the side of a stretcher.

Mike, sitting on the end of the table, pulled a mouth-organ out of his shirt pocket, and began playing 'Maria, Mari'. It was as if he had heard her wish.

Tears came into Maria's eyes; the music made her almost painfully happy. She sang softly:

> *'Speramo ce parlar'* . . .
> *Mari, oi Mari!'*

To hide her tears, she got up and said she had better begin preparing the meal. Mike wandered to the kitchen door after her, still playing. Then he put the mouth-organ in his pocket and lit the stove for her.

Maria tried to pick up too many eggs at once, and

103

one rolled on to the floor and exploded like a small bomb. She stood clutching the rest of the eggs helplessly to her breast, staring at Mike in distress, two large tears still in her eyes. Ah, how clumsy! What would he think of her?

Mike thought that she looked very sweet and appealing. He took the eggs gently from her, put them down on the little table, and folded her in his arms.

'Don't be upset,' he said. 'Don't you know that we have a proverb: "You can't make omelettes without breaking eggs"?'

'But not on the *floor*!' Maria's voice was muffled. 'I am so—*mi vergogna . . .*'

'Well, it *is* better to use a bowl . . .'

Then they both began to laugh. She looked up into his face, and he kissed her laughing mouth, and her lovely eyes, still wet and tasting of tears. His arms tightened round her. The stove purred quietly.

Just then there was a crash as the front fly-wire door was flung back. They jumped apart; Maria began feverishly breaking eggs into a bowl.

Mandy's voice sounded wearily: 'Well, thank God! My poor feet! It must be nearly a hundred miles from the river by your damned short cuts.'

'Nonsense! You're soft, that's all. Just because you're used to driving everywhere—'

'I am making omelettes!' called Maria gaily.

'And I'm breaking the eggs,' said Mike.

There was a small, stunned silence from the other room, then Mandy gasped: 'Mike's here!' and fled towards the mirror.

But Mike was already stooping through the kitchen doorway.

'Hullo girls, I'm afraid you weren't expecting me. Mandy *did* ask me to tea a couple of weeks ago, and I thought it was tonight.'

'Hullo, Mike. We're glad to have you,' said Mitch.

Mandy looked at him silently. She knew that her hair was a mess, that she had no lipstick on, that her face was shiny and sweat-streaked, her legs and arms scratched from the lignum bushes Mitch had led her through. And here he was, in a white shirt and a plain tie, a well-cut sports coat and perfectly creased grey trousers; she had never seen him looking so handsome, assured and well-dressed. And at the corner of his mouth was a little smear of lipstick.

She turned blindly towards the mirror, groping for a brush. Her jealousy of Maria was like a physical pain in her breast. Now that she was sure that she had lost him, she wanted Mike more than any man she had ever known.

Mitch went through to the kitchen to wash her hands and help Maria, who was, she noticed, looking remarkably pretty and animated.

When she had brushed her hair and dashed on some lipstick, Mandy felt a little better, though she was tired from the long walk and knew her face looked drawn. She turned towards Mike and said in a low voice:

'You might have waited for me.'

'I did wait. I've been here over half an hour.' He handed her a cupful of beer, and poured another for himself. He was being wilfully obtuse.

'You know what I mean.'

He was enjoying for once being master of the situation; but before he could reply Mitch came in

105

and flung herself on her stretcher.

She waved her hand at the thick white cups on the table. 'Come, fill the Cup . . .' she murmured.

'Beer or gin, Mitch?'

'Oh, a beer please, Mike! I've got a thirst as long as the Murray. How thoughtful of you to have turned up with all these lovely bottles.'

He poured another drink for Maria and took it through to the kitchen. She looked at him with shining eyes. A light golden omelette was steaming in the pan. Maria was sorry she had no herbs or cheese to flavour it with, but the natural flavour of the butter would have to do. Australian butter was tasty and salty, she was beginning to like it very much.

Over the omelettes and the beer they all became quite gay. Mandy had recovered her poise, and was the gayest of them all. Maria, who had finished her third gin squash, was inclined to giggle. Mitch gave an imitation of Rosie's performance with the blancmange, and Di-anne's discomfiture, which reduced them to helpless shrieks of laughter. Mike brought out his mouth-organ and played.

The night, instead of becoming cooler, grew hotter and more oppressive. Moths and flying-ants made a cloud about the lamp, for the wire screens did not fit properly. The ants shed their wings and went crawling about looking for cracks in which to found new colonies.

Mitch, going out to empty the teapot after making tea—for Mike and Maria had washed up, and Mandy protested that she was too tired to lift a finger—saw that the whole sky had clouded over. There was not a star to be seen, and it was breathlessly still.

'Feels a bit like a thunderstorm coming,' she said as she re-entered. Mike looked worried for a moment.

'Hope not,' he said. 'Rain now might ruin the gordos and sullies if we don't get a drying wind after it. And some of the currants are spread in the open.'

'Won't the roofs protect the sultanas that are already on the drying-racks?' asked Mandy.

'Not if the rain drifts at all. I'd have to let down the weather-curtains. And of course, if you leave them down too long the fruit goes mouldy.'

'Mold-y?' asked Maria.

'Yair—whiskers all over 'em, you know. And I'm the one who's held responsible. The poor bloody foreman is responsible for everything, except the weather; and they've got an idea that even that's my fault.'

He told them about the year when a stray monsoon wandered down from the north and lingered about the river towns for a week. The fruit still on the vines cracked, and was then sucked dry by ants and bees; the fruit on the racks sprouted whiskers long enough to shave. Only a fraction of the usual hundreds of tons was exported that year; and some of the smaller growers faced ruin.

Other years there were droughts, when the river fell below the level of the pumps, and had to be dammed; or the lock-gates were opened too soon and millions of gallons of life-giving water flowed away and were lost in the sea. Then would come a flood so high that the pump-house was inundated, and the vineyards as well, and when the waters receded they left a saline deposit leached from the soil, which began to kill the vines and fruit trees.

107

Then of course there were plagues of caterpillars or snails, and the menace of odium and block-rot; of severe frosts damaging the young shoots in spring.

'Always something interesting happening,' said Mike with a grin.

Tap! Tap-tap-tap!

Something hit the iron roof like a hail of small pebbles.

Mike sat tense and alert. A sudden gust of warm wind banged the wire door to and fro. There was a feel of dampness in the air.

Tap-tap-tap! Tap-tap-tap! Then a steady drumming on the galvanised-iron roof.

'Hell! Rain!' Mike was on his feet instantly. 'My hat—? No, I didn't bring one. Sorry, girls, but I must sprint. I'll have to get the currants under cover. Thanks very much for the meal.' He was at the door.

'Wait! Mike!' Maria had dashed to her corner of the room, and was already tying a scarf over her dark hair, dragging on a raincoat, 'I am coming to help you, I am not tired.' She glanced at Mandy, daring her to deny that she had just said she was too tired to move. 'I am strong, I do not mind the rain.'

While Mike was still protesting, Maria dashed out of the door ahead of him and ran to the car. She was rather amazed at herself. She had lost all her timidity, and felt strong and sure and wise.

'Well! What's come over our little Maria?' Mitch said wonderingly. 'How much gin has she had, do you suppose?'

Mandy did not answer. She had flung herself on her stretcher with her face to the wall. 'She really must be exhausted,' Mitch thought.

Mandy was silently reviling herself. Why hadn't

she thought of offering to help Mike? It was she who should be out there with him in the warm darkness. Always something went wrong or came between them. Why had she tired herself out walking back from the river?

And then, when he drew out the mouth-organ just now, after tea, she had not been able to repress a tiny shudder of distaste, sure that he would play some dreadful pop tune . . .

He had begun a sensitive rendering of Schubert's 'Serenade'. Though she didn't like mouth-organs, she was pleased at his skill.

'I didn't know you were musical,' she said, and felt that she sounded condescending.

He had looked at her rather mockingly, tapped the instrument on the palm of his hand, and said: 'There are quite a lot of things you don't know about me.'

She was tempted to puncture his unusual complacency, to say: 'I know something you don't think I know, about your grandmother,' but she couldn't do it. Instead she had turned away, pretending indifference. He began to play an Italian song for Maria; and when Maria asked her to sing, she refused.

Mandy groaned and bit the pillow.

'Why don't you get right into bed, Man?' said Mitch, sympathetically. 'You'll be more comfortable if you get undressed before you fall asleep.'

She mumbled something in reply, pretending to be half-asleep already. But her every nerve was stretched taut: the rain drumming on the iron roof seemed unbearably loud.

CHAPTER THIRTEEN

Oh, Thou, who didst with Pitfall and with Gin
Beset the Road I was to wander in,
Thou wilt not with Predestination round
Enmesh me, and impute my Fall to Sin?

Mike drove fast, saying little, feeling Maria's worshipping gaze on his face in the dim light. Here was a mess! The girl had probably never been kissed before, regarded it as a sort of betrothal. There had been no time to speak, to dismiss the moment of tenderness into which he had been surprised, with a light word and a laugh.

As they turned into the gate and drove along the track of the other property towards the racks, he took one hand from the wheel and clasped hers that were lying in her lap.

'Look, Maria, I shouldn't have done that—kissed you, I mean. You're only a kid, I know. But you looked so sad and funny when you dropped that egg, and I suppose I wanted to comfort you.' At the same moment a sharp memory came back to him of the softness of her lips, of her shoulders, and he knew that he wanted to kiss her again. Hell! He glared at the rain which flew towards the windscreen like a handful of flung spears, or a shower of meteors from a radiant point somewhere ahead.

'You are wrong, Mike. I am not a child. I am married. My husband, he is dead.'

'Maria! I'm sorry.' He stopped the car by the racks, but for the moment the fruit was forgotten. 'I had no idea! You look so young.' The scarf over her hair framed her face, hid the abundant hair, made her look suddenly more mature. He squeezed her hand and got out. Maria tumbled out the other side.

'I'll get a hurricane lantern alight.' They ran to the shed, and he struck matches and found the lantern on a shelf, full of kerosene. Then together they went out into the rain. He had put a clean sack over his shoulders to keep off the worst of it.

Only two days before, Mitch and Mandy had spent the afternoon spreading and rolling out the great heaps of dried currants on the hessian ground-sheets into which they had been shaken. They were now almost ready to be tipped into the sweat-boxes and carted off to the co-operative packing-sheds for cleaning and packaging. The rain was falling directly on to them.

Mike threw canvas covers over the larger heaps, and together he and Maria dragged the smaller ones to shelter. Then they let down the weather-curtains on the windward side of the racks where the sultanas were already turning golden and wrinkled.

They were just in time, Mike said. No damage would be done as long as the rain did not go on for days, and a drying wind came up by the morning. Maria looked at the rain slanting in golden lines past the lantern, at Mike's figure as they sheltered in the lee of a rack. She felt strangely exhilarated by their isolation in that circle of dim radiance, all around them in the night, the silence, the darkness and the warm rain.

'Thank you, Maria,' he said gently. 'You were a great help with those heaps of currants. You must have strong arms.'

'*Si*. I have strong arms.'

Her eyes were only pools of greater blackness in the night, he could not see the expression in them; but he understood the note in her voice. He turned abruptly on his heel. 'I must put the lantern away, and take you home.'

She followed him into the shed, and put a hand on his damp sleeve. 'You are wet, you will be cold.'

'No, I'm not cold a bit.' He set the lantern down, but before he put it out he stopped, arrested by the look on her face. She was staring at him with great luminous eyes in which her love showed plainly.

'*Ahi*, Mike!' She took his hand and pressed it to her lips, and then to her breast, inside the stiff raincoat. Mike stopped thinking entirely. Somehow she was in his arms, her damp scarf fallen back from her hair, and he was kissing her eyelids again, which no longer tasted of salt tears, but of rain.

Lord, how soft! You forgot how soft a woman's body could be... He was remembering with his hands, with his lips, like a blind man re-discovering a once-familiar territory. It was years, two years since a girl had been his, and all because of his wilful pride, which had messed up yet another affair; that, and his fear of being trapped...

'Maria! Darling!' He raised his head and looked questioningly into her face. She looked back serenely. With a quick movement he lifted her from her feet and laid her on the pile of hessian in the corner. She lay with closed eyes, smiling. He could hear nothing but the thunder of his own heart.

Her face and throat were wet with rain, and in his

nostrils was the sweet scent of earth receiving the blessing of moisture from the sky. He felt like a god possessing the warm, fecund earth.

* * *

Back in the car, he sat a moment before switching on the engine, his arm around her shoulders, his lips in her hair. He felt both peaceful and guilty.

'Dear Maria, why did you tell me that fib?'

'Fib? Oh dear, what is "fib"? "Fig" is a fruit, this I know—there is a tree outside the door of Mrs Binks's and they grow also in Italy. At home, we—'

'Maria! Stop talking. I think you know very well what a fib is. It is a lie.'

She said in a small voice: 'I do not tell lies.'

'You told me you were married, or had been married, and your husband was dead. But you are a girl still: or were. I can tell, darling. I am the first, isn't it so?'

'It is so. But I was married, by proxy, to Mario Delcalmo. He died before my ship arrives in Australia. So, you understand, I am married yet I am not married. I am a widow before I have been a wife.'

'Poor kid!'

'And I am not a "kid"!'

'No; you are a woman now. Maria, I'm sorry—'

'You are not sorry; you are happy. It is you who tell fibs.'

He laughed. 'Yes, I'm happy. And you're lovely.'

He started the engine. Maria leant on his shoulder with a happy sigh. Yet she was faintly uneasy. He had not said one word about marrying

113

her. And she loved him so!

*   *   *

'Never again!' groaned Fred, as he helped Merv and young Alf to unload the full tins from the cart, and stack them beside the dip. 'Gurh, I feel awful. Can't understand it, I never drunk nothin' but wine. Not as though I was mixing me drinks or anythink.'

'What did yer do to yer face, Fred? Spoilt yer beauty a bit, 'aventcher?'

'Dunno,' said Fred mendaciously, fingering his scored cheek. 'Must of run into a barb-wire fence, I s'pose.'

'Or a rose-bush, per'aps?' said Merv, with a wink at young Alf.

Fred ignored this, and they unloaded the rest of the tins in silence, and piled a load of empties back on the cart.

Mitch, watching from up on the rack where they were now spreading on the third layer, several feet from the ground, saw horse and cart disappear between the rows of vines as into a green sea. The rack was like a jetty; and from it she saw Fred and Alf borne along over the waves of the vines as if by some miraculous process; they were like old Triton and some attendant merman, and she half-expected, at the end of a row, to see emerge a boat of mother-of-pearl drawn by dolphins, instead of the rickety cart and the prosaic form of Peanut.

Peanut, lusting after sultanas, made a nuisance of himself at lunch-time, and had to be tied up well away from the racks. Now, towards the end of March, there was beginning to be a nip in the air, a touch of autumn. It was cold if you were not actually in the sun. All the pickers began gathering round the dip-fire at lunch-time, toasting their sandwiches or boiling billies.

Mitch, asking after the health of the gloomy Myrtle, was answered by Big Alf:

'Oh, she's not too good at present. It's the Change comin' on her, yer see.'

'Oh, er, I see,' said Mitch, supposing that as a married woman she must expect these confidences. 'My husband is coming up next week-end,' she said brightly.

'That'll be nice, love. A real second honeymoon, it'll be. Alf an' me, we always go away together every year, on our annivers'ry. Last year we was snatchin' potatoes down in the south-east; next year we're goin' hop-pickin'.'

Mitch ground her teeth. What did this middle-aged shapeless pair know of love? She and Richard were young, and they should be together. Oh, why couldn't they get a house? She closed her eyes and saw quite clearly Richard's slim hips and waist, his broad shoulders and smooth, hairless chest; and turned faint with desire and longing. Oh, Richard, Richard!

She was lonely for him, among all the companionship of the other girls; for Maria seemed to have some secret happiness of her own into which she had withdrawn; while Mandy was in one of her moods, silent and glum, or flaring up over nothing.

*   *   *

Mike had taken the spark-plugs out of the tractor to

115

clean them.

'Where they dirty, Mike?' David was leaning forward with his hands on his little grubby knees, inspecting the spark-plugs lying in a clean handkerchief. Mitch whipped out her pencil and sketch-pad, catching his pose while he was intent and still.

'The points are dirty, these pieces of wire here, see? When they're dirty they won't make a spark, and the engine won't go.'

The rain had blown away quickly and left no ill effects. Some of the sultanas were already dry. They had been shaken down that morning and spread on sheets on the ground.

There came a roar from Merv, who came charging along the rack, brandishing the dip-strainer in one huge fist.

'That ruddy 'orse!' he shouted, belabouring Peanut. ''E's eatin' the dried sullies now.'

Peanut had browsed right across a sheet of hessian, leaving a clean wake. Mike rushed to help Merv, and Peanut, snatching a last mouthful, ambled off.

When Mike came back he was met by a cheerful David, clutching the handkerchief to his breast, in which reposed six dripping wet spark-plugs.

'I was'ed them for you, Mike,' he said. 'They'll 'park in a minnut.'

'Oh, Davey! You naughty boy!' cried Mother Mac, but after a moment of consternation Mike gave a shout of laughter.

'Thanks a lot, old man,' he said, taking the bundle of wet plugs. 'You're a great help round the place.'

Maria looked at him tenderly. He was so good

and kind! And she had been so frightened of him, that first day, when he got cross with her for picking every grape off its stem. She belonged to him now, and she was glad. If he beat her every day, she would still want to be his.

David went up to Mandy, asking from habit: 'Where's your watz, Mandy? Is your watz broked? What time does it say?'

Abstractedly she held out her left wrist to him, but he kept piping: 'Where's your watz, Mandy? Where's your watz?'

'Oh, for heaven's sake, David,' she said irritably. 'It's on my wrist, of course.'

'No, it's not!' his voice squeaked with excitement. 'It's not on your writz. Is it broked?'

Mandy looked at her wrist, and gave a small scream. 'It's gone! My watch!'

'You can't have put it on this morning,' said Mitch.

'But I did! I know, because I checked it when the seven o'clock whistle blew, just after breakfast. I had it on then.'

'It must have fallen off when you were spreading.'

'Yes. Maybe.' She looked at Maria. 'Or maybe not. As Mrs Jordan says, pickers will take anything.'

'Mandy!' Mitch stared at her. 'If anyone found it, they'd hand it back to you, I'm sure.'

'Maybe,' said Mandy again. Maria moved uncomfortably under her stare.

'Of course they would,' said Mitch crossly.

The missing watch threw a blight over their hut. That night Mitch and Maria searched, while Mandy ostentatiously did not. 'You won't find it,' was all she would say. 'It's not just that it's a valuable watch, but it was my mother's.'

'You shouldn't have worn it on the block,' said Mitch.

'I thought it was safer than leaving it here.'

Maria took a deep breath and said carefully: 'Mandy, do you perhaps think that I—?'

'Oh, what rot, Maria!' interrupted Mitch.

'I think nothing,' said Mandy. 'It's gone, and there is no use talking about it.'

They went to bed in silence, and there was none of the usual light-hearted chatter after the lamp was out.

CHAPTER FOURTEEN

Ah, Moon of my Delight, who know'st no wane
The Moon of Heav'n is rising once again:
How oft hereafter rising shall she look
Through this same Garden after me—in vain!

Mitch was glad that a full moon coincided with Richard's visit to Vindura. She was convinced that she was sensitive to the moon's phases much as the sea was, and like those sea-creatures of sub-tropical waters which come to the surface to mate only on the night of full moon, she became restless and excited and unable to sleep on such nights.

He arrived by plane on Friday afternoon, and Mitch left work early to go and meet him. She'd had to tell Rosie Binks that she would not be in to meals for the next two days, and had endured the inevitable reference to 'a second honeymoon', with

118

a terrifying leer from Rosie's battered face. Mandy and Maria were coming to the hotel to dinner with them on Saturday night.

At the Community Hotel she spread her few things round the room, making herself at home.

'Oh, it's lovely, Richard! What luxury—three whole rooms!' She opened the door once more into the white-tiled bathroom, and peeped again into the sitting-room. There were wall-to-wall carpets, soft and thick, and full-length mirrors.

He caught her as she went flitting past, and folded her in his long arms. He looked over her head at their reflection in a wall-mirror. She was a little thing, but full of vitality. He closed his eyes and felt her well-remembered shape, smelled her remembered perfume. He removed his glasses and peered at the large bed.

'That bed,' he said. 'It *looks* all right, but I think we should just try it out, don't you . . . ?'

*   *   *

Mitch woke some time after midnight and knew at once that Richard was with her. It was as if they had never been apart. They had gone down to dinner and had what seemed a wonderful meal after Mrs Binks's cooking, and a bottle of wine with it. And then . . . 'There's a picture on at the local theatre if you want to see it,' said Mitch.

They looked at each other and laughed, and went straight upstairs after coffee. They had a bath together in the gleaming sunken bath like two children, and went back to bed.

Mitch lay and looked at Richard, who had rolled away from her and was sleeping peacefully on his

119

back, his long legs spread half across the bed. In the moonlight coming through the big french windows she could see his light, tousled hair, his gentle mouth and closed eyes. He had his lost, little-boy look without his glasses. She resisted the impulse to kiss him, he must be tired after his journey.

Instead she slipped quietly out of bed and went over the soft carpet to the french windows that opened on to the balcony, with a view over the river. She undid the latch, and the light of the full moon streamed whitely into the room. Below lay the hotel garden sloping down to the water's edge.

'Oh!' breathed Mitch. She could see a great curve of the river gleaming under the moon. The smell of water and trees came up to her, the throaty chorus of frogs, the strange, hollow cry of water-birds. She stepped forward, forgetting the high step, and landed on the balcony with a crash and a cry of agony.

'Oh! My toe, my toe!'

Richard was with her in a moment, half-awake.

'I've never seen such a clumsy idiot,' he said crossly. 'What did you go and do that for?'

'I couldn't HELP it. I was just going out on to the balcony, and there was a step.'

'Of course there was a step. The step was there this afternoon when we went out to look at the sunset. I believe you like knocking yourself about.'

'Richard!' she wailed. 'You might show a bit of sympathy. I think my toe is broken.'

He lifted her up and carried her inside, and they examined her left big toe in the light. It was already turning blue and beginning to swell.

'Not broken,' he said, waggling the bone. 'You've sprained it, that's all. I'll make you a cold

120

compress.'

He bound the toe carefully with a wet face-cloth, his hands gentle and deft. He was properly awake now, and in a better temper. He comforted and caressed her until she forgot the pain in her foot, and at last fell deeply and peacefully asleep in his arms.

*   *   *

On Monday morning Mitch came trailing in to breakfast last. She was tired, and depressed because Richard was gone and it was nearly two months before she would be returning to him. She limped perceptibly, for her toe was still swollen and painful.

'Oh-oh!' cried Rosie, who was just setting the teapot down on the table. ''Ere comes the bride! Eh, look at her, Fred. Second honeymoon too much for yer, love? Never mind, a good strong cupper tea'll set you up.'

'I had a fall at the hotel, and sprained my toe,' said Mitch with dignity.

'Sprained 'er toe! 'Er *toe*! That's a good one. Ha-ha-ho-ho-ho!'

Mitch just restrained herself from casting the sugar-bowl at Rosie, and gave a long-suffering smile to the others. She was worried about the future of their little group, for Maria and Mandy had scarcely addressed each other at dinner the other night. This morning they seemed more cheerful, but this may have been because they were going to see Mike today. She had a shrewd idea of how Maria felt about Mike, and that Mandy would like to cut her out. There was more than the

121

incident of the missing watch behind their hostility, she felt sure.

Mandy, for her part, was determined not to give up Mike without a struggle. He had so nearly been hers, up to that night by the Lock when she had behaved so foolishly.

She would like to begin wearing a dress to work, like Maria, so that he could see her to more advantage; but after all, he had seen her in a bathing-costume, and presumably his imagination and memory were adequate. She decided on a piece of active strategy.

They were now working on the topmost layer of the rack, hanging on somehow with their elbows while standing on a plank. Mitch, because of her injured toe, found difficulty in climbing up, and was set to stoking the dip, unloading full tins, and stacking empties ready for the cart to pick up.

Mike, who often helped the spreaders when a heavy load came in, or when they had spread a load of dipped fruit just before lunch or smoke-oh, stood beside Mandy and rolled the wet bunches across the wire-netting. Sometimes their gloved hands touched. It was both disturbing and delightful to have him so near.

He got down to tighten a sagging layer, standing just below. Mandy looked down out of the corner of her eye, gave a small scream, and stepped with apparent artlessness off the plank.

It was high enough from the ground for her to have injured herself quite badly. It was a calculated risk she took, and he did not fail her. He turned and caught her in his arms, staggering at the impact to regain his balance.

'I told you to be careful!' he scolded, still holding

her in his arms.

She looked up at him, unsmiling. 'Oh, Mike!' she said softly. His eyes travelled over her lovely face and dwelt upon her mouth; he kissed her with his eyes, not his lips. The trolley was coming back with a load of dipped fruit, and he set her gently on her feet.

'Mike!' she cried again. 'I want to see you, alone. I must see you. There's something I want to tell you. When?'

'I don't know. Saturday—' He looked away, towards the approaching trolley pushed by Tom and Dick.

'Saturday, then—at five, I'll be down by the river, just below the wharf. We always go into town on Saturday, and I'll give the others the slip.'

'All right.' He looked both pleased and troubled. When the trolley came he did not climb up again beside her, but went back to the dip to help Mitch.

*   *   *

Maria had dreaded the thought of going to Confession, yet she knew she would feel better when she had told her sin and been absolved.

She had not seen Mike alone since the night of the thunderstorm; he had not suggested that they should meet, or that he should come to the cottage. Perhaps he was feeling ashamed of himself, sorry for what had happened? It had been her fault, really. She did not know what had come over her; perhaps she'd had too much of that drink which looked like lemon squash. She was glad this time that Mike was not in the church.

She trembled as she knelt in the confessional and

123

heard the priest's stern questions: 'It has not happened again? Do you truly repent of your sin?' and at last heard the words: 'Go in peace, my daughter, and sin no more.'

Now she felt better, picking in the cool early morning sunlight opposite Mother Mac, while young David crawled to and fro through the vines. The sultanas were trellised, but not nearly as high or thick as the currant vines, so that she could see her partner's kindly wrinkled face and her spectacles flashing in the sun as she worked.

There was a certain satisfaction in picking sultanas, for the bunches were so big and fat that only a few were necessary to fill a tin. But the piece-rates had dropped by half, so that she did not earn any more money.

She was beginning to feel that she had always lived in Vindura, Australia, as though her other life had been a dream; a dream dreamt only last night, still clear in her memory, but belonging to a different order of reality. Because Mike was here she could not imagine living anywhere else. What was she to do when the grape-picking season was over? Perhaps she could get a job in the packaging factory for the winter. She would have to ask that Mr Pike, the one Mitch said was 'drongo'.

Her happiness had been ruined for the time being by the loss of the watch. Mandy showed that she was suspicious, in all sorts of little ways. No one would believe that Maria had not stolen it; even Mitch must be wondering. What if the police came for her? Perhaps she would be sent back to her own country . . . She knew for certain now that she did not want to go. Since she had worked close to its soil, she felt that she belonged to her adopted land.

Then an incident occurred which made her feel, in spite of her worry over the watch, that the other workers were really her friends, her 'mates' as they called it. People who worked together were mates, and they always stuck up for each other.

It was Merv who first told the story, walking up from the dip to the shadow of the racks at lunchtime, with a great vein standing out in his brown neck, his hairy fists clenched.

'It makes me bloody wild!' he was muttering.

'What does, Merv?'

'No drinkin'-water, that's what!'

'Water! Didn't know yer touched the stuff. Now if it was beer—'

'No, but these Eyetalians over on Pike's other block, they got three little kids and a baby, see? And no fresh water, because old Pike was too flamin' mean to let 'em have any. 'E said they could drink the water out of the channel—stagnant stuff left from the last bloody irrigation. Now they'se come out all over sores, and bloody well 'ad to go to 'orspital.'

'Shame!'

'He shouldn't be allowed to get away with that.'

'I suppose they could have boiled the channel water,' said Mandy.

'Perhaps they're living in a tent, with no proper stove,' said Mitch.

'They'se livin' in a caravan, just here for the season. There's a bloody great three-thousand gallon tank on the shed near them, but Pike reckoned they'd waste the rainwater.'

'She would have much washing, the poor lady, with four *bambini*,' said Maria.

'Well, what say we send a deputation to old Pike,

saying if they don't get a fair bloody go we stop getting the crop in? The winter's comin', and he wouldn't like the grapes to stop on the vines until it rains, now would he?'

'I'll be in on that, mate.'

'You've got to show 'im 'e can't get away with that sort of thing.'

'All in favour? Righto. Now I'll just send round the hat. Any little contributions gratefully accepted. We should rake up enough to pay the bloody doctor's bill, anyway.'

Maria was amazed to see the pile of silver coins growing in the hat, on top of a crumpled ten-shilling note put in by Merv. They were giving money for a family they had never seen, a family of Italians; but they were fellow-workers. She dropped in her own contribution. Mandy pulled a folded pound-note out of the pocket of her jeans and added it to the pile.

'Officially, I'm supposed to be on the bosses' side, but here's my bit,' said Mike adding a handful of loose coins. Merv grinned, his tombstone teeth flashing beneath his broken nose.

'She's jake,' he said. 'Pike'll climb down, 'e's a bloody gutless bastard. I'll go over an' chat him this arvo. Who else is comin'? You, Alf? And young Joe? Good on yer.'

CHAPTER FIFTEEN

And this delightful Herb whose tender Green
Fledges the River's Lip on which we lean—
Ah, lean upon it lightly! for who knows

Mandy did up the buttons down the front of her brown-and-white striped cotton dress, with fingers that were clumsy with excitement. She wore a necklace of white shells, which showed up the eggshell-brown of her bare neck and shoulders. Her hair was brushed and sleek, gleaming like a golden helmet.

She frowned a moment, noticing her bare left wrist and the tiny pale line where the watch-band used to protect it from the sun. She slipped a matching shell bracelet over the wrist. A mere dash of powder over her fine, smooth skin, and a generous amount of lipstick on her ripe-looking mouth, and she was ready.

Instead of trying to shake off the others after they reached the town, she had decided to let them go on without her, saying that she was tired and was not going in to do any shopping that afternoon. Then she would catch a later bus and go straight to the wharf to meet Mike.

Such small lies did not worry Mandy; she told them automatically and habitually, so that they almost came more naturally to her than the truth. Yet she had been telling the truth when she said that she wanted to see Mike alone to tell him something. She wanted to tell him that she knew about his quartering of dark blood, that it meant nothing to her, that he should not be ashamed of his ancestry. She would have to be very tactful. Yet she felt that there should be no secrets between them, and if he would not tell her himself, she must broach the subject . . .

She saw him at once, standing by the water's

127

edge, casually dressed in slacks and an open-necked white shirt. He seemed to sense her coming, for as she approached noiselessly over the sloping, lawn-covered bank he turned and smiled up at her.

It was hot down by the river, which was not rippled by the faintest breeze, but reflected the sun dazzlingly from its smooth surface. Mike had a small boat pulled up to the bank, the oars ready in the rowlocks. He asked her if she would like to go for a row on the river.

Mandy was delighted. She hadn't wanted to stay in the centre of the town, where they might run into Mitch and Maria at any moment. She stepped in expertly, not rocking the boat more than necessary, but also not dispensing with the strong arm he put out to steady her. 'Gosh, you look lovely,' he said sincerely.

She sat on a thwart and arranged her full skirts gracefully, but not too decorously, showing a frill of lace on her stiffened petticoat and a pair of smooth brown legs. Mike averted his eyes modestly as he sat opposite her to row, looking over his shoulder for direction. Mandy laughed with excitement. She had him all to herself, and even if Maria were here, she felt she could have held her own. Maria was charming to look at, but she had no style, thought Mandy complacently.

Mike rowed competently; the dinghy skimmed over the water smoothly and silently, but for the regular click of the rowlocks; the oar-blades flashed wetly in the sun as they turned. Mandy's heart settled down from its wild beating, and seemed to throb in time to the regular back-thrust of the oars. She relaxed happily, closing her eyes against the glare of the sun. Through her lashes she saw Mike looking at her.

'Where are we going?' she murmured.

'Up-stream. The Lock's in the other direction. Besides, there's something I want to show you.'

They were silent for a while, and then he said: 'You're very brown. You didn't get that tan all in one season, I'll bet.'

'No ... I do a lot of swimming at the beach. You're very brown, too.' She opened her eyes and looked at him quizzically.

'Yes ...' Mike looked away, and missed a stroke with one oar. He recovered the rhythm quickly, but she saw that he was ill at ease. Now was the time to speak.

'I wanted to tell you—' they both began together. They stopped and laughed, and the tension was broken.

'Never mind. It can wait,' said Mike.

'Yes. So can mine. What a perfectly heavenly afternoon!'

They had rounded a bend and were already out of sight of the wharf, the Riverside Club, the Hotel gardens and the many moored launches and houseboats of the town, though they still passed private landings among the willows, and fishermen's cottages with drum-nets lying about the doors. They could see the almost imperceptible current flowing between the pillars of the big bridge as they passed underneath—only the second bridge in four hundred miles of river, which elsewhere had to be crossed by punt, or car-ferry.

Now the green willows gave place to grey box trees and the sombre blue-grey and brown-olive of gum tree foliage, the land's original flora,

129

unchanged since it first became a separate continent. And now, too, the land's original inhabitants, or some pathetic remnants of them, came into view.

Mandy saw that they had reached a point near where she had come on the 'pickernic' with Fred and Rosie Binks. Ahead, on the far side of the river, she saw the miserable humpies and the drawn-up dinghies of the blacks' camp. There was no smoke today, and it had a deserted and desolate air.

Perhaps she had been wrong about Mike. He couldn't be very sensitive on the subject of his relations or he would never have brought her in this direction. She glanced at him, and saw that he was looking at her intently. He shipped the oars and let the boat glide on with its own momentum.

'I've often felt,' he said, wiping the sweat from his forehead with his shirt-sleeve, 'that you were disappointed in me, that night when we went out to the Lock. You wanted me to stop and talk to your social friends; you wanted me to be one of the mob.

'Well, I'm not; and I brought you here this afternoon to tell you why. You see those huts over there? That's known as Pinky Flat, where the natives and half-castes live—'

'Mike! I—'

'Wait a minute. "Pinky", in case you didn't know, is another name for "plonk", or the cheap wine that they get drunk on. They're not allowed to buy alcohol, of course, and anyone selling it to them can get pinched. But they never have any trouble getting it—at a price. And there doesn't seem to be a place for them, in the white man's civilisation, to do anything else but drink. They drink to forget their hopeless position.'

'It's shameful! Why, the land belonged to them first. And now they're not even allowed to live in the town, or have decent houses—'

'How did you know that? Anyway, there they are: outcasts in the country where their ancestors hunted for thousands of years, not allowed to live on the same side of the river as the white people. And my grandmother was born over there, lived there until she was married. Now you know.'

'Mike,' said Mandy softly, 'I knew already. That's what I wanted to tell you, that I knew and it didn't matter.'

'You mean you've known all along?'

He began to row again, mechanically.

'Not all along. I didn't know that night. But I'm glad I know now. I think it's—it's rather romantic.'

'Romantic! Hell!' He rowed a few vigorous strokes. 'My grandmother married a quarter-caste who lived in the town, and my father married a girl whose skin was not as dark as yours. But everyone knows. You said that night I had a chip on my shoulder. Do you wonder? Descended from a "dirty, demoralised—"'

'Yes, I wonder at you, Mike. A man of your intelligence, to adopt the mental attitudes of the Jordans and the Pikes of this town. How clean do you think Mrs Jordan would look if she was forced to live in a bag humpy in the bush? I'd just like to see her. And that putrid little Di-anne! As for being demoralised because they drink, I'd say most Australians, the men, anyway, drink too much. These people are unhappy, they don't fit into either world, Sydney or the Bush. As you said, they drink to forget.'

131

He rowed with new energy, while looking at her admiringly.

'Mandy, you're amazing! I didn't expect you to understand. I just wanted to end a false situation. Besides—' He was thinking of Maria; and whenever he remembered that night in the store-shed a pang of guilt went through him.

'I suppose, coming from the city, I have a different point of view. Actually the only aborigine I'd ever seen was a singer, a full-blood from the far north. He had the most wonderful concert platform manner and superb natural dignity. I was most impressed.'

'That's different. An artist will always find his own level. But—for instance—would you have considered marrying him?'

Mandy dropped her eyes and flushed a little. 'Why, I don't know. I've never thought about it; never thought of such a thing. One would have to consider the possible children—'

'That's not quite what I meant, but never mind.'

'If you meant, did I find him attractive, the answer is yes—I can quite understand Desdemona.'

They rowed on in silence. Mandy turned to trail her fingers in the water over the bows. She had suddenly found his intent scrutiny embarrassing. 'Don't forget we have to row back again,' she murmured.

'We could always drift with the current; but it would take a long time.'

They had rounded another bend, and now the camp and the last vestiges of the town had dropped behind them. Mike made for a clean spit of white sand running down into the water on the inside of the next bend. He beached the dinghy with a soft scrunch, jumped ashore and pulled it up higher. Mandy stepped to the beach dry-shod.

The sandy bank was fretted with sharp-carved lines showing the different levels the water had reached. It slowed up to a levee bank crowned with tussocky grasses and skinny tobacco-bush, and was strewn with fallen leaves and twigs, strips of smooth bark, and small, woody fruits from a great red-gum growing at the water's edge.

The huge root system spread partly over the surface of the ground. Half-way up the trunk was a large black excrescence, a kind of diseased growth distorting the tree's symmetry.

'They call those nigger-heads,' said Mike, pointing. 'Ugly things!'

'Hush! Mike.' Mandy put her hand over his lips. 'You don't have to wear your chip with me.'

He pressed her hand against his lips, then her wrist and elbow, and bent his dark head to kiss her bare shoulder.

'My love!' he said. 'I love you, Mandy. I've never known anyone like you ... Ever since you fell off the cart that day ...'

'And I had to fall off the rack as well before I could get you to admit it.'

'You mean you fell off there on purpose? You mad girl, you might have broken your neck! Don't ever do anything like that again. You're too lovely, too precious, too beautiful ...'

She closed her eyes and let his wild words flow over her, like balm to her scarred and homeless spirit. When his lips found hers at last she was half fainting with happiness. 'I must sit down, Mike. You make me feel hollow-kneed.'

He lowered her gently to the warm sand, half in the shadow of the great tree, and sat beside her, gazing tenderly at her face, her lips, her closed eyes. He pushed the soft hair behind one ear and traced its outline. With trembling fingers he smoothed the curve of her brows, the faint hollow of her cheek.

There came a high-pitched, mellow trumpeting, and Mandy opened her eyes to see two black swans flying down the river, low above the water, their long black necks outstretched, their white wing-tips beating. At each downstroke a double flash of white was reflected from the surface. They glided down to land at the end of the reach, one behind the other, setting up a wake of foam, and then sailed about with arched necks. At that distance they were more than mere birds, symbolic, heart-rendingly lovely. Foolish tears started to her eyes. Once more a mood of melancholy threatened to defeat her.

'Good Lord!' She was startled out of it by Mike's vigorous exclamation. 'The dinghy! I didn't fix it properly, and it's floated off. Oh, hell, it isn't mine either, or I'd let it go.'

They gazed after the dinghy, which had drifted to mid-stream where the current was strongest. It was beginning to float back the way they had come.

'Sorry, Mandy, but I'll have to go after it.' Mike stood up and began stripping off his clothes. She sat with her hands clasped about her knees and watched as, clad only in his brief underpants, he made a running dive and swam strongly after the truant boat. He guided it back to shore without attempting to climb into it, and this time fixed it securely with a clove-hitch round a projecting root.

She looked appreciatively at his lithe brown limbs and muscular shoulders, but she said, mocking at them both: 'Just like Alan Ladd! He always manages to strip off before an admiring audience.'

'Ah, come off it! D'you think I did it on purpose?' He turned his back on her and began pulling on his clothes. The moment of tenderness was gone.

She laughed, seeing his small boy's scowl as he turned, struggling with a shoe. She was not to know that all his boyhood he had gone barefoot, until his father had suddenly decreed that he must never go out without shoes on again: 'That's how the black kids go about. My kids have got to act white, see?'

She leaned over and touched his hand. 'I was only teasing you. Why are you so touchy, Mike?'

'I am with you, because I'm not your sort. I know you're only amusing yourself with me.'

'Mike, that's not true! Do you want me to prove it to you? Let's stay here, I'll stay with you all night if you like. As a—as a sort of an act of faith.'

He lifted her to her feet and kissed her, but his face was troubled. 'You see, I didn't tell you . . . I'm really not a practised Don Juan, but the fact is . . . Maria—'

'Maria!' Mandy recoiled slightly. 'You mean—?'

'I'm afraid so. I feel terrible about it, honestly. She's such a child in some ways, but I thought she'd been married before, and—oh, hell! I felt I ought to tell you that she has a sort of prior claim on me. It was you I wanted really, it was you I loved all the time, but you seemed hostile, and—'

'And Maria threw herself at your head? Oh, I know, I've seen the way she looks at you. What a mess! And I was feeling so happy, it's so peaceful

135

here.' She flung her arms round his neck. 'Let's forget there is anyone else in the world.'

He gently detached her arms. 'No, we'd better get back. The chap wants his boat at sunset. I'll have to see Maria and straighten things out, tell her about you. Poor kid! She'll take it pretty hard, I'm afraid.'

Mandy bit her lip, hard. She was not used to being refused, and the sweetness of desire was beginning to turn sour with keeping. On the row back she only just managed to conceal that she was in a terrible temper. For the time being she hated Maria.

CHAPTER SIXTEEN

And look—a thousand Blossoms with the Day
Woke—and a thousand scatter'd into Clay:
And this first Summer Month that brings the Rose
Shall take Jamshýd and Kaikobad away.

Autumn had come upon Vindura by imperceptible degrees. The mornings were colder, the sun rose later; distances were softened by a blue frost-smoke which hung in the air until nearly midday.

The young poplar trees had turned to pencils of yellow flame, and at each gust the leaves were scattered like sparks. Maria felt in tune with the season as she looked at the sad, sodden gold drifted along the drive. Her hopes were falling one by one like withered leaves.

Yet the vines were still green and vigorous, she noticed as she walked between the rows of gordomuscatels which they had been picking since the sultanas cut out. She liked eating the luscious muscatels, with their pulpy flesh in clear globes big enough to be taken in two bites; but they had large, bitter pips.

She took a bunch with her, as she went up to the dip at lunch-time, to eat with the rather unsatisfying sandwiches that Mrs Binks prepared. Mother Mac had gone off among the higher rows with David, who always had to be helped when he wanted to relieve himself. She met Mike at the end of the row, and they walked together along to the dip.

He laughed as she screwed up her face over the tart, astringent taste of a pip she had just bitten into. There was a clever machine at the packing-sheds, he told her, which removed the pips while still leaving the dried raisins almost whole. They were then just right for making plum-puddings and mince-pies.

He explained that a plum-pudding had no plums, and a mince-pie no meat, and that they were eaten as an accompaniment to roast turkey and ham at Christmastime. (She had never known an Australian Christmas, as she had spent hers with the Italian family in Melbourne.)

'They are all the same as *antipasta, si*? Meence-pie and plum-pud'?'

'Well, I don't know. What is *antipasta*?'

'In Italy, we have before the meal, to commence with. Olives, perhaps, or ham and melon, or anchovies in oil. *Pasta* is spaghett', macaroni, ravioli—*antipasta* we eat before the *pasta*.'

'Er, no, that's what we call savouries. These others are sweet, and pretty solid. I'd like to try

137

some of this Da—Italian food, though I don't think you can beat good old steak and eggs.'

'I would like to cook for you.'

Oh, hell, thought Mike, how did I get into this? He remembered the omelette she had prepared for him that night. It had been a jolly good omelette, too. He said impulsively: 'No, I'd like to take you out to a meal. There's that new Italian café in the town, I've never been there. What about coming on Saturday? And then we could go to the pictures afterwards if you like.'

He owed her that much, at least, he thought. He felt even more uncomfortable about the rôle he was playing when he saw how she reacted. Her whole face shone as though lit up from within; her dark eyes became luminous.

'Oh, Mike! Just me? You want to take me to dinner?'

'Sure, Maria.'

'I would like to come very much.'

'Then I'll meet you at Rizzoni's at six, shall I?'

'*Si*—I mean yes. It is Ritz-zoni's; that is how it is pronounced in Italy.'

'Ah! Like the Ritz?'

'*Come?*'

'Skip it.'

To his surprise, Maria flushed crimson. She gave him a startled, resentful look and began hurrying away.

'Maria! What's the matter?' He gripped her arm and swung her round to face him. She stared at him with dark, angry eyes.

'You told me to go away.'

'You're mad. I asked you out to dinner.'

'And then you said, just like that: "Hop it!" That

138

is how young Alf speaks to David when he is being a nuisance.'

'I didn't say "Hop it", I said "*Skip* it." It's quite different. It just means forget it, it doesn't matter, it's not worth explaining, never mind. See?'

'Oh, of course! I am so stupid, I will never learn.'

'You're not stupid, Maria. It takes time to get used to these slang terms.'

They had walked on and reached the racks, and now Mandy came sauntering up to them, pulling off her rubber gloves, her bare head shining in the sun. She gave Maria an unfriendly look, and said to Mike, ignoring her:

'I've never found my watch, you know. I suppose it hasn't turned up anywhere on the block?'

'No, I'm afraid not. It could be buried in a furrow, with sand kicked over it by now.'

'It *could* be,' said Mandy. Maria flushed again and walked away.

Mike looked after her in surprise, and turned back to Mandy. 'You're not suggesting, by any chance—?'

'Well, what am I to think? To a girl like that, a watch of any sort would be a temptation, and mine was a pretty one, set in sapphires and diamonds.'

'I think you misjudge Maria. She strikes me as simple, sincere, and honest as the day.'

'No doubt you should know,' said Mandy. Her face was set in cold, obstinate lines.

She's a bitch really, a rich bitch, he thought, unblinded for the moment by her charm and beauty and sheer animal attractiveness. Then, as they walked along to the dip side by side, in silent hostility, her arm brushed his. The fine down of hers just brushed the dark hair on his forearm, and

139

an electric current of attraction flowed between them. He could no longer look at her objectively.

Mother Mac came along with Maria and Mitch. They were talking about hospital, to which Mrs Wilkes's husband had been carted off the day before with appendicitis.

'Only real 'oliday I ever 'ad was in hospital,' said Mother Mac, 'I was in there a month, and I got me hands that nice,' she said, looking at her cracked and stained fingers regretfully. 'They never been that nice again. Almost sorry to leave I was, if it 'adn't been for them bed-pans.'

'I have never been ill,' said Maria. 'But on the boat, coming from Italy, I had a holiday. It was too long with nothing to do. I was, how you say, "sick of it".'

'You could give me a bit of that kind of sickness,' said Mother Mac. 'A boat, eh? And all your meals served up in style, and no washin' up . . . I've got to cut five lunches, and get breakfast, and milk the cow, every morning before work, and there's always a bit of washin' and ironin' at night, as well as the weekly wash, and I got to do that on Saturdays. Young Davey gets his clothes that filthy—Where *is* Davey, anyway?'

She stopped with a sandwich half-way to her mouth to look round anxiously. Just then came the wail of a train whistle from the road, and a train went clanking past. Mother Mac went white. She struggled to her feet.

'David! David!'

There was no answer. The others looked round helpfully, telling her not to worry, but Mother Mac was clucking like a disturbed hen. He had gone back to get his teddy-bear, which he had left sitting in a tin under the vines, and she thought he was following her.

There was no sign of him at the racks or in the sheds. Alarm began to spread when they had all called for five minutes without result. Even Slow Joe stopped chewing like a ruminant cow and gazed about short-sightedly.

'We'd better organise a search,' said Mike. 'Now, Mother Mac, calm down and tell us exactly where you saw him last ... Right, we'll search between the racks and the north fence. Each take a row, and look carefully all the way; he's probably just gone to sleep under a vine. When you get to the end, walk down the fence to the road; if no one has found him, we'll spread out along the channel—'

'The channel!'

'It's all right, Mother Mac, there are fifty acres of vines he could be lost in. Don't start imagining the worst.'

'Come, drink some tea,' said Maria, handing her a cup. 'Then come with me, and we will search together.'

By the time the pickers met at the road fence there were plenty of worried faces apart from Mrs MacGowan's. They had called and beaten right through the section of vineyard where David had last been seen. Mandy kept thinking of the train-line, Mitch of the deep water in the main channel, Maria of the snakes lurking in the ditches. David's mother saw a hundred dreadful possibilities in as many seconds.

'I shouldn't of let him go back alone! I shouldn't of let him!' she wailed.

'Do not blame yourself, *cara madre*. We will find him all-a-right.'

They began to spread out along the channel which ran just outside the fence. Then Fred Binks, who was in advance, gave a shout. The others ran up to find him standing up to his chest in the channel water, holding a small, limp form in his arms.

''E was on the bottom,' he said hoarsely. 'Poor little bastard! 'E's a goner, Mike,' he whispered, as Mike knelt on the channel edge to take the burden.

Mrs MacGowan flung herself forward with an agonised cry. She snatched the boy from Mike's arms with extraordinary strength, and began kissing the cold, bluish cheeks, the lank hair and closed eyes, crying as though she would bring him back to life with her warm tears.

'Alf! Run up to the house and get them to ring a doctor,' said Mike urgently. 'Tell Mrs Pike to get a bed ready, and fill it with hot-water bottles. I'll carry him, Mother Mac . . .'

'Wait!' The others, standing round in numb horror, started at Mandy's imperious tones. 'We ought to try artificial respiration at once. There's not a minute to lose. Mitch, you know the routine; we did life-saving at school. We'll take it in turns, but we mustn't stop for a moment.'

Mrs MacGowan, beside herself, seemed disinclined to yield up the little boy, but Mike gently persuaded her. Mandy ran a finger round the boy's throat to feel for any obstruction of food, held him up to drain the water from his lungs, and then laid him face down on the warm earth, his head turned to one side. She began the rhythmic movements of artificial respiration, counting slowly, with intense concentration.

If the others had expected a rapid miracle, they

were disappointed. A quarter of an hour went by, and Mitch took over; a half an hour, and Mandy took her place again. Alf came back to say the doctor was just leaving. He brought two hot-water bottles. Maria tried to comfort Mother Mac, as she sat rocking herself with trembling lips, almost as pale as the child on the ground, his cheek pressed to the rich, red, sandy earth.

Mike stood tensely by. 'You must be tired,' he said to Mandy. 'I could do that.'

'I'm going to try something else. Let's turn him over.' As they did so they noticed a faint colour in the cheek that had been undermost. 'I believe he's responding.'

Kneeling, she held his nostrils closed with one hand, and putting her lips to the boy's mouth, breathed steadily into it. His chest rose perceptibly. Again and again she breathed for him. Gradually a pink colour replaced the terrible blue of asphyxia in his face; the lids stirred, and he gave a little whimpering cry. His mother began to massage his feet, kneeling in the red sand and sobbing with relief. Mandy put her ear against his chest and heard the steady beating of a small heart.

The doctor, hurrying down the track, met a subdued but triumphant procession bearing a David fully restored to consciousness, and a mother who, with shock and reaction, needed his treatment too. He congratulated Mandy on her swift action; she was the heroine of the hour. She had just time to notice that he was young and good-looking, before he bundled the patients into his car.

After lunch, Mike declared a holiday for the rest of the day. They would just help him shake down a rack of sultanas and then go home. So they bounced the wires with a will, and the wrinkled, golden sultanas fell to the hessian, leaving only a few dried stems clinging to the wire-netting.

'What's that?' cried Mitch, pointing to a small, glittering object that was left on the third layer. Tangled among the wire, and bound there by a dried and twisted stem, was Mandy's watch.

'It must have fallen off while you were spreading, and been covered by the bunches. Look, it's not hurt at all!' She handed it to Mandy, who wound it up and heard its faint but sturdy tick, like the beat of that little heart which she had set going again today. She had felt a strange, godlike power, a creative glory such as a doctor must feel when he has saved a life which otherwise would have ended prematurely. She would like to have been a doctor.

'A reward for your courageous action today,' said Mike.

'I've had my reward already. It was when I heard his heart begin to beat.'

'I am so glad it is found,' said Maria beside her.

Mandy turned, and gave her a smile of spontaneous warmth and charm. 'Thank you, Maria. I'm glad too.' She did not say: 'I am sorry for my suspicions, and for making you miserable,' but she put out her hand and Maria clasped it happily, knowing that this was what she meant.

CHAPTER SEVENTEEN

Ah, my Beloved, fill the Cup that clears
TO-DAY of past Regrets and future Fears—

144

To-morrow?—Why, to-morrow I may be
Myself with Yesterday's Sev'n Thousand Years.

Immediately after they were dipped to remove their natural coating of wax, the gordos took on a beautiful iridescence. Mitch liked to roll them gently into place, and see them lying like globules of blown glass, like pale-green Christmas tree ornaments, on the wire.

They had just finished spreading a load, and she was dreamily watching a flock of galahs perched in an almond tree near the sheds, looking like a cluster of exotic blossoms with their rose-pink breasts all turned towards the faint breeze. There was a clatter and a shout behind her, and she turned to see Dick hold up a tiny, buff-coloured field-mouse by the tail. He had just discovered a nest beneath a loose sheet of galvanised iron.

'Let's put it down her neck,' he said to Tom, advancing on Mitch with a gleam in his eyes. It was the first of April, and all sorts of practical jokes and leg-pulls had been going on during the morning.

'I'm not frightened of mice, as it happens,' said Mitch. 'Only, let the poor little thing go.'

Disappointed of their sport, they paused and looked about. 'I know! Let's drop it in the dip,' said Tom.

They went over to the steaming copper with its brick chimney, at the moment left unattended by Merv, and Dick held the squeaking mite above the hot caustic solution.

'*No!*' cried Mitch, and flew at him like a tigress. He raised his arm high above his head to hold the mouse beyond her reach.

She grabbed at his arm, and the mouse was

145

jerked from his grip and fell straight into the scalding liquid.

'Oh, you beast! You hateful beast!' cried Mitch, in rage and horror.

'Hell, I didn't mean to drop it in really. You knocked it out of me hand.' Tom looked rather sick, but Dick was grinning.

Mitch turned away with tears in her eyes, and went back to the rack. 'Why didn't you help me get it from him?' she demanded of Mandy, who was leaning composedly on the wire.

'All that fuss about a mouse!' said Mandy.

Mitch said nothing, but her face was white. It was not the first time she had noticed a certain hardness and lack of sympathy in her friend.

Fred Binks had suffered most during the morning. He had got down to lift the last two tins of grapes from the end of a row, and the first one nearly broke his back; it was lined with stones and clods of earth, with a few bunches on top to disguise them. At the next tin he tensed his muscles and heaved, and the tin flew up into his face. It was filled with paper, leaves, and grass, similarly disguised.

His temper was not improved by this, and when he noticed the pickers pointing and laughing each time he drove past in the cart, he began to look down his heavy nose with a black, sullen stare. At lunch-time he discovered that young Alf had pinned a paper to the back of his singlet with the legend:

I AM THE
BIGGEST GRAPE
ON THIS BLOCK

146

'I'll flatten yer!' he roared, shaping up to young Alf; but Mitch sprang between them and quoted from *The Magic Puddin'* in ringing tones:

> Oh let the fist of Friendship
> Be kept for Friendship's foes;
> Ne'er let that hand in anger land
> On Friendship's holy nose!'

This so astonished Fred that he sat down and stared at her, while young Alf discreetly disappeared for the time being.

'That's from *The Magic Puddin'*,' she explained to Maria.

'This magic pud'—is it a plum pud'?' asked Maria, proud of her knowledge of Australian foods.

'It's a plum-pud', or a steak-an'-kidney pud', or any other kind of pudding you want. It's a *magic* pudding, and it can talk, and it runs away from its owners if they don't keep it shut up in its basin. It is a famous character of Australian literature; as famous as Renzo in *I Promessi Sposi*—'

'Ah, you have read Manzoni!'

'Only in translation, in English.'

'He was a great writer,' said Mandy politely. 'They say, do they not:

> *Un tempio e un uomo,*
> *Manzoni ed il Duomo.*'

'*Si*, in Milano, where he was born. The *Duomo* is the greatest church in Italy. I have seen it once, on my way to catch the boat in Genova.'

'I should like to see Milan cathedral,' said Mandy musingly. 'I've always wanted to go to Italy; once I thought I would go there to study singing, and perhaps sing one day at La Scala, but I wasn't good enough for that.'

'You would like the opera there,' said Maria.

'Why don't you go? What's to stop you?' said Mitch. 'You could afford it. I'd go like a shot, if—'

She paused, thinking of Richard, with his pipe in his mouth, sitting by their very own fireplace with a book. Beyond the circle of light from the reading-lamp was a wicker crib trimmed with blue satin bows, and a round, downy head was just visible on the pillow . . . Broody! She was definitely getting broody. And yesterday she had felt rather queer in the morning. Her heart beat with sudden excitement, mixed with dismay. If only they had a house! She just wanted one small piece of the world to call her own.

'I don't know. I suppose I'm just lazy,' said Mandy. 'And then, I've usually been involved with my life here.' Her eyes rested on the lean figure of Mike Hannaford, who was talking to Merv beside the dip.

They were discussing the Italian family on the other block. They were out of hospital again, and the baby had no sores because the mother fed it herself. Pike had agreed to let them use the rain-water tank until the end of the season, which was only a month off.

That afternoon Mitch and Mandy spread and turned tons of sticky sultanas as they lay on hessian sheets in the sun. They delved up to their elbows in the golden fruit, but they were not tempted to eat any. Queer bugs and beetles crawled among the

148

heaps, and Mitch kept thinking of the mouse, which had been fished out of the dip with all the hair gone from its body. 'And people *eat* sultanas!' she said, shuddering.

'She would refuse to eat anything, probably, if she saw the whole manufacturing process,' said Mandy wisely. And, anyway, Mike had said the fruit was all washed and treated at the packing-sheds. 'I'd rather eat sultanas than sausages, any day,' she said. 'Mysteries, they call them.'

'Sausages were the only things I could cook when I got married. Oh, and boiled eggs. How I'd love to have a kitchen of my very own! You know, I've half a mind to have a baby straight away, and then we'll *have* to get a house,' she said disingenuously. She was not going to let Mandy know she hadn't planned it, if her suspicions proved correct. She meant to slip in to see a doctor in the town next week-end.

'M'm. Good idea,' said Mandy absently. She was wondering how she would like cooking for Mike, in some little house in Vindura. Not so little; her father would help them, buy him a block of his own with a house on it and give her a handsome dowry as well. She would be quite content . . . at least, for a time. But she could not imagine living away from the city for ever.

'Blue-and-white checked gingham for the kitchen curtains, I think,' Mitch was saying.

'No, red-spotted muslin, and a plain red linoleum . . .'

Mandy's voice trailed away. She had suddenly remembered something, something Maria had told her. Wasn't Mike a Roman Catholic? And her father, intelligent and open-minded as he was in most directions, had this one blind spot, his prejudice against Roman Catholics. He would never agree to her marrying one. If she did so she would have to forgo money, dowry, possibly even her inheritance, unless Mike would give up his faith. She had no idea how strongly he held to it, but Maria said she had seen him at Mass. She would have to find out very tactfully. She sensed an obstinacy and strength of will in him as great as her own.

*   *   *

Mike filled Maria's glasss from the bottle of *vino rosso* on the table.

'*Salute!*' she said, looking into his eyes.

'Your health, *signora*.'

'*Prego*. But please—*signorina*! I am not married any more. I wish to forget the past.'

'To the future, *signorina*.'

Oh, how could she tell him? The future was bound up with him; he did not know, but she knew, she was almost sure, that she was carrying his child.

'Did you like the *pasta*?' she said lightly.

'Not too bad—what reached my mouth, that is. Now I'd like something solid—'

'Like steak and eggs? Then, cutlets of veal, with green salad and fried potatoes; and after, *cassata speciale*.'

'What's that?' asked Mike suspiciously.

'A kind of cake made of ice-cream, with cherries and almonds and raisins—'

'You don't expect me to eat dried fruit, do you? After seeing it in the raw all day?'

'This is very nice, you will like it.'

150

Mike found the veal rather thin, he couldn't get his teeth into it like he could into a piece of steak, but it was very tasty and tender, and the potatoes were excellent. The bottle of wine was empty. He ordered another.

Maria was animated, her usually slumberous dark eyes sparkling. She had been talking in her own tongue with the waiter, and was surprised to find how easily the words flowed, after two months of disuse. He came from Bergamo, a little town not far from Milan; he had been in Australia two years, and he did not want to go back. He missed most of all the music, the open-air cafés and the opera; and then the processions, the feast-days of the church. But he liked this country, and his youngest boy had been born here, a real Australian.

When he had gone back to the kitchen, Maria said: 'I, too, miss the church; it is different here. I have not seen you at church lately, Mike. Perhaps you have not been to early Mass?'

'No, but I must go tomorrow. Will I see you there?'

'*Si, si*—I mean yes.'

'Perhaps we could go for a walk afterwards.' For Maria was looking so charming in the soft light, with her pale blue dress and rippling dark hair, her eyes alight with love and the joy of being near him, that he could not stop looking at her. He was enjoying the meal, but when it was finished he still felt hungry. He called the waiter.

'He is still hungry,' said Maria, laughing. '*Ha fame. Questi Australiani hanno i grandi appetiti!*'

'Some fresh fruit, signor? We have-a da nice grapes—'

'Hell, no!'

151

'Some *minestrone* for the *signor*, perhaps?'

'What is it?'

'Soup. Thick soup, with many vegetables. You like.'

By the time he had finished the soup Mike admitted that he had had enough. As he sat sipping the aromatic coffee he thought of the usual accompaniment of steak and eggs; stewed tea, or 'coffee' made with essence and boiled milk, with a skin on top and an over-cooked taste. A few more cafés like this one might educate Australians into demanding, and getting, something better. The wine had been Australian, light and dry, but it had given him a pleasant glow. He picked up the bottle and said musingly: 'The fruitful grape . . . you can have it fresh, or dried, or fermented; whole or crushed; with pips or without; solid or liquid. A remarkable food. What do you call it; in Italy, I mean?'

'*Uva*.'

'*Uva*? Isn't that an egg?'

'No, *ova* means egg.'

'*Uva, ova, pasta, minestrone* . . . I'll be talking your lingo soon. *Andiamo*, Maria!'

'*Andiam*', Micaelo.'

The first feature had begun when they arrived. After the interval there was a turgid romance about a girl with masses of dark hair who looked rather like Maria, and who got her man in the end after the complications necessary to spin out the story for one and a half hours.

He found himself watching Maria rather than the screen, as she sat beside him in silent absorption. Once, carried away by a tense moment, she gripped the arm of the seat between them. He covered her fingers with his, and half unconsciously they twined about his hand.

He was still holding her hand when the lights went up. He had quite forgotten to watch the screen. Looking round he saw Mandy a few rows behind, staring at him rigidly. She gave no sign of recognition, but turned and pushed her way out of the theatre.

He realised that for a considerable time he had not given Mandy a thought. Yet he was in love with Mandy, he told himself, not with Maria. He had meant to be friendly, brotherly and kind tonight, to indicate that he was sorry for what had happened and that it must never happen again. And what must Mandy be thinking by now?

Then, when he drove Maria home, she lifted her face so naturally to his that it would have been churlish not to kiss her; and her mouth was so soft that he found himself kissing her again. By then it was too late to make the brotherly speech. He would have to tell her somehow after church. Meanwhile he felt sure that she regarded herself as engaged. How on earth was he to tell her?

CHAPTER EIGHTEEN

How long, how long in infinite Pursuit
Of This and That endeavour and dispute?
Better be merry with the fruitful Grape
Than sadder after none, or bitter, Fruit.

On Sunday afternoon the three girls swam in the rather murky waters of the dam. Maria was becoming more daring, and declared that she would not be afraid to swim in the river now. But Mitch, thinking of the new life she carried, felt that her own was more precious than ever before. She preferred to swim in the dam where she could drop her feet to the bottom if she had to. However slimy and unpleasant, it was at least solid. David's accident in the channel—he had gone there looking for 'fogs', he told his mother—had made her nervous.

Preoccupied as she was with her own affairs, she noticed that Maria and Mandy were very quiet. They had been quite friendly again since the incident of the missing watch was cleared up; but yesterday when Maria announced that she was going out with Mike, Mandy's brow had become thunderous; and last night she had gone off by herself. Today, she hardly spoke, but lay inert on a towel, soaking the sun into her long brown limbs.

Maria's arms and legs were just as smooth and brown, though more sturdy and less slender; but her neck and shoulders were still white. She covered them with a kerchief to save herself from getting burnt.

Mitch lay on her back and squinted down her chest at her flat stomach. It was hard to believe that she would soon be shapeless, just an enormous bulge from the waist down. She had always been so small and slight that she could not imagine herself large and unwieldy. She was not going to like it, she felt sure.

She had resisted an impulse to wire Richard straight away. He might ring her tonight, anyway; and she would rather wait until the doctor confirmed what she suspected. At least he must see now that they had to get a place of their own; her parents-in-law were too old to be bothered with babies in the house.

Mandy was sitting up, yawning and rubbing at her wet hair, and announcing that she was going over to the house to wash it. The Jordans had just gone out for a drive, and she meant to have a shower while the she-dragon was away.

'Don't forget to mop the floor,' murmured Mitch. 'Dry it as you would a plate . . .'

She rolled over on her face, listening to the gentle whisper of wind among the restlessly turning leaves of the poplars. They seemed to be sighing and complaining, in an autumn melancholy: 'Our life is brief, brief . . . our youth is over, age is upon us, and soon we fade and fall. . .'

'What is that song, about "youth is ever fleeting"?' she asked Maria. 'You know, the one Mandy sings, Lorenzo's song?'

> *'Ah quant'è bella giovenezza*
> *Che si fugge tuttavia—'*

'Yes, that's it: How beautiful is youth, which flees . . . What would you say,' she added abruptly, 'if I told you I was going to have a baby? At least, I *think* so. I'm thrilled, really, but it's a sort of an ending. Life will never be the same again.'

Never . . . Never . . . Never the same, sighed the poplars tremblingly.

'Oh, Mitch, that is wonderful! Richard will be so pleased, will he not? And so proud. Oh, Mitch!' and Maria began to sob.

'Maria!—What's up? Is it Mario?' She rolled over and put an arm round the shaking shoulders.

155

Maria's face was buried in her arms. 'You mustn't be sad. You'll marry again and have lots of babies—'

'Oh! Oh!' moaned Maria. 'That is the trouble! I am not married, and I am ashamed ... *mi vergogna* ...'

'You mean ... you mean, you too? We are both—' Well!' Mitch pondered for a moment. 'Is it—is it Mike?'

'*Si*. And I love him, I want him to be the father of my *bambino*, but he has not asked me to—to marry him, and what shall I do?'

'Does he know about it?'

'No, no. I could not tell him.'

'Then I will!'

'No, no!'

Mitch stared under her wet hair at a blackened, rotting gum-leaf floating on the surface of the dam. Here was a mess! She felt somehow responsible for Maria, alone in a strange country. Mike, she felt sure, would marry her if he knew. But how much was he involved with Mandy? And would Mandy give him up?

'I am surprised at Mike,' she said at last, her voice severe. 'You, a young girl, alone, without friends or relatives ...'

'It was my fault! You do not know! He has thought I am already married once, and I—I— It was when we went over to cover the sultanas. Last night, he bring me straight to home.'

'I should think so! And he hasn't mentioned marriage?'

'No,' said Maria, and added in a small voice: 'Mandy is very beautiful, *non è vero?*'

'I'm going to have a word with Mandy,' said

Mitch.

'You would not tell her! And perhaps she loves him also.'

'You don't understand, Maria. All men are fair game to Mandy. She wouldn't be happy till she'd taken him from you; but once he was hers, his value would drop immediately. I think I can persuade her to leave the field. And Mike is really fond of you, anyone can see that. He wouldn't have asked you out last night otherwise.'

'You think so?' Maria sat up and smiled through her tears.

'I'm sure of it. And I think you'd make him a wonderful wife. Mandy is a city girl, through and through. She would never fit in here. Look, I'm going to the doctor on Saturday, why don't you come with me and we'll both be examined?'

'Oh no!'

'Yes. You must make certain, and you should have a check on your health. Meanwhile, you stay here and have a sunbathe and I'll go and chat with Mandy. She'll be back at the cottage by now ... This must be a terribly fertile district,' she muttered, walking along the red sandy track beneath the dramatic sky in which the clouds, long and flat-based, with their silvery tops and strong purple shadows, looked unreal as clouds in a technicolour film. 'I expect I'll have twins, at least! "Fruitful as the vine," they say.'

Mandy was sitting on the ground by the back door, leaning against the wooden wall of the cottage, with her head down and her damp golden hair spread in the sun.

'Mandy, I want to talk to you. About Mike.'

'Mm?' said Mandy lazily. 'What about Mike?'

157

'Is he in love with you?'

'Why? And what if he is?'

'If you're going to tell me to mind my own business, I regard this as my business. I feel responsible for Maria, she is the youngest of us—'

'What has it to do with Maria?' Mandy looked up. Her eyes were greenish, guarded.

'Everything. She is going to have a baby.'

'Oh.' She bent her head again.

'You have to give him up, Mandy. You know Mike would be in love with her if it weren't for you. He got her into this mess, and I'm sure he'd marry her if he knew, but that's not enough. He has to *want* to marry her, or she'll never be happy.'

'And what about my happiness?'

'You know you will console yourself before too long. It doesn't go very deep with you; it's just a way of passing the time in this small town. To Maria it's her whole life. Mandy, you've got to listen!' For she had dropped her fair head again and Mitch thought she was almost asleep. 'You must convince Mike that you were only amusing yourself. You must make him hate you, if necessary. But we have to get him to propose to Maria.'

Mandy looked up, and to Mitch's intense surprise her eyes were full of tears. They looked shadowed and tragic.

'I love him, Mitch. He's the first *real* person I've ever known. I would even live in Vindura for the rest of my life, to be with him.'

Mitch goggled at her. 'I believe you really would.'

'Yes! And supposing I were to tell you that I am in the same condition?'

'Oh no! Not all three of us.' Mitch sank down beside her and began to giggle. It was suddenly more funny than tragic.

'No, not really. Why, are you—'

'I'm almost sure. I'm going to the doctor on Saturday.'

'Congratulations,' said Mandy dryly.

'It has me worried, rather. But I expect I'll feel very maternal once it actually arrives—the baby, I mean.'

'Yes, nature has a way of looking after these things, I imagine.'

'But Mandy, what are we going to do? Here you are both in love with Mike, and apparently he has managed to seduce Maria (and I don't blame her, for he's certainly very attractive), and for all I know he's seduced you too . . .'

'What do you mean, seduced? Don't you know the proper word? Don't be so old-fashioned; you sound like a virtuous mill-girl in *Mary Barton*.'

'Well, anyway, the fact is that Maria simply has to get married, and you don't. And it would be very apt really, wouldn't it—I mean, an old Australian, descended from the very first Australians, marrying one of the newest of New Australians?'

'But why should I help her? Why should I cut my own throat?' She turned and beat against the wall with her fist. 'I love him, I want him more than I've ever wanted anything, and I believe he loves me . . .'

'Why did you work so hard to save that child's life?' asked Mitch softly.

Mandy got up, keeping her face averted.

'I'm going for a walk,' she said. 'No, don't come with me. I want to think.' And she walked away

159

between the long perspective rows of the vines, in the opposite direction from the dam.

Mike had still not managed to have an explanation with Maria that morning. The longer he left it the harder it became for him to speak. After Mass they had walked along the river-bank in the clear sunshine, and Maria had told him of her mother and brothers and sisters in Italy, and how sometimes she longed to see them.

For a moment a way out of his dilemma leapt to his mind. 'Would you like to go back, Maria?' he had asked. 'Do you want to go back to Italy? Perhaps—'

'Ahi, no, Mike! Never! I love ... I love everything here too much. This is my country now. How can you ask? Never could I go back.'

All her feeling for him was in her soft dark eyes, in the agitated rise and fall of her breast under the demure white lace blouse. After that he couldn't blandly suggest that perhaps she would find another husband among the Italian community, that he himself was not the marrying kind, that there was someone else ...

And he couldn't help feeling responsible for her. He had been the first ... And Italian girls were carefully guarded. Perhaps none of her countrymen would want her now.

After he had left her he walked away out into the saltbush country, to the barren, sandy hills where only the belars grew in sombre strength. A warm wind keened among the drooping fronds with a sound of long-lost seas.

The wind moaned, over and over: 'Man—dy! Man—dy!' echoing the cry in his mind. He was fond of Maria, but Mandy was a fever burning in

160

his blood. He wondered, for the hundredth time, what had come over him that afternoon when the dinghy floated away. She had been there, in his arms, offering to stay with him all night, and he had worried about getting the dinghy back on time!

The sudden cold dip had damped his passion, and his feeling of guilt over Maria had come between them. Oh, if he had her here now, under this tree, in the warm red sand! But Mandy at that moment was walking, away over on the other side of the settlement, between the rows of vines that turned about her like the spokes of a great green wheel.

CHAPTER NINETEEN

And when Thyself with shining Foot shall pass
Among the Guests Star-scatter'd on the Grass,
And in thy joyous Errand reach the Spot
When I made one—turn down an empty Glass!

Mitch wired to Richard:
INSIST ON HAVING OUR SON IN OUR OWN HOME
STOP LETTER FOLLOWING LOVE MITCH
It didn't occur to her until after she had sent it that now Richard would enlist her mother on his side, and demand that she come home and not endanger the future heir of the Fairbrothers by climbing on racks and spreading grapes.

The doctor had confirmed her suspicions and also Maria's. There was not the slightest need for her to give up her job, he said; exercise in the open air was good for her and would keep the baby

161

small, but she must not go on to the point of exhaustion.

Talking to Mrs Wilkes during smoke-oh the next day, Mitch realised that Maria was perhaps fortunate in being in Vindura rather than the city in her predicament. It was a tolerant community where such things were concerned, and many families of now respectably married couples had been begun in the soft, warm sand of the river-bank.

As long as marriage followed within a year, there was no stigma attached to the child or the parents who had somewhat anticipated the wedding.

Mrs Wilkes confided that she was worried about her daughter, Daisybud. She wanted to get married to a young man in the town, an apprentice who was really not earning enough to marry on, but Daisybud wanted to marry and take a job as well.

'Why don't they wait until they've saved a bit?' she complained. 'What they want to get married in such a hurry for? It's not as though they had to. Dais is not in the family way or anythink. I can't see no point in it. A young wife shouldn't be working.'

'Then you think I should be home with my husband, not working as a picker?' asked Mitch.

'Too right! If I was him I'd come up and take you home. Money's not everything. A wife's place is with 'er husband.'

'I suppose you're right,' said Mitch meekly.

That night when Richard rang she was more ready than usual to listen to his appeals; but she couldn't go home now and leave Maria in such a fix, she must get things sorted out. She couldn't explain all this on the phone, with Mrs Jordan hovering in the background and Di-anne openly

162

listening.

Richard sounded excited, anxious, and incredulous; he kept asking was she sure, and insisting that she had better come straight home. 'If you don't come by the end of the month,' he said ominously, 'I'm coming to get you. And you won't be going back.'

'I'll write to you,' was all Mitch could say. 'I'll write you a long letter and explain.'

*   *   *

Mandy had walked for miles on the Sunday afternoon, and had come home exhausted in body and mind; for her mind travelled round and round in circles, and always came back to the same impasse: she loved Mike, but she could not marry him, and if she kept him from marrying Maria she would be acting like a dog in the manger.

Her father, she knew, would never agree to her marrying a Roman Catholic, so she could not count on a settlement from him. She was used to spending money without thinking; and she had sufficient cynicism—or good sense, whichever it should be called—to know that love in a cottage would begin to pall after an idyllic year or two.

She imagined herself with several babies, doing all her own cooking and washing ... nappies drying round the stove, messy meals in the kitchen, yelling children ... No, such domestic joys were not for her.

She had made one or two mocking remarks about religion to Mike, to test the depth of his faith. 'It must be very comfortable,' she said one day, 'to be able to sin freely and then go to the priest and confess and be absolved, as you do . . .'

'That's not true!' said Mike. 'I never confess. But I believe in the Church. My mother was a devout Catholic, and she made me promise to follow her faith.'

Mandy said no more. She knew that his mother was dead, and that he would never break a promise to her.

But how could she give up Mike? She felt that she could not live without him. And would he consent to being given up? She was sure he had meant it when he said he loved her. And yet, last night, she had seen him holding Maria's hand, gazing at her face. Supposing he really loved her all the time? Mitch took it for granted that Mandy only had to lift a finger to make him her slave. But she herself felt a nagging doubt. Her uncertainty increased her love, her longing to win him wholly.

She believed that she could do it; after all, he had not asked Maria to marry him. Yet she shrank from putting it to the test. And Maria, when she came back from the doctor, had looked so tragic, so pale, that Mandy felt alarmed in case she might wander away and throw herself in the river.

She must not be responsible for another self-sought death like her mother's. Mandy felt an odd personal guilt over that long-ago tragedy which she had been too young to understand or to prevent. She felt that if only she had been older, if her mother had been able to confide in her, it might not have happened.

Now someone's happiness, perhaps whole future existence, lay in her hands. 'You will have to make him hate you, if necessary,' Mitch had said. 'He has to want to marry Maria, or they'll both be miserable.' Mandy came to her difficult decision. She would convince Mike that she did not love him, even hurt his pride so that he would turn to Maria for solace.

The opportunity did not come at once; she had no chance to speak to him alone, for he was busy getting the last of the crop away to the packing-sheds. The following week, the picking on the first block being completed, they began working on the home block, among the vines round the Jordans' cottage.

Mandy had developed hay-fever again, for the day was warm and blowy, with thin streamers of cloud teased out across the blue. She went to get a scarf to tie over her nose and mouth, thinking how Mike had given her his handkerchief two months ago for a mask.

Mike, who had been longing to get her away from the others, and yet felt it would be unnecessarily cruel to Maria to invite her openly to meet him (for he had not yet plucked up courage to tell her of the 'other girl') had to go up to the big house to see Bob Jordan. He hurried along the track and caught up with Mandy where the trellised vines hid them from the pickers.

Mandy looked at him with swollen eyes which were not entirely due to hay-fever; she had scarcely slept the last few nights, and had heard Maria tossing and turning as restlessly as herself.

'You poor darling,' he said tenderly. 'That rotten hay-fever again! I'd better come up to the cottage with you and fix on your scarf.' He grasped the hand nearest to him and interlocked his fingers with hers, just caressing the inside of her wrist with his thumb. Mandy breathed more quickly, but managed to leave her hand limp and unresponsive in his.

His washed-out blue shirt was open at the neck showing his brown throat; the whites of his eyes were clear with health. Her heart turned over with love. At least my eyes look terrible, Mandy thought with a corner of her mind. That may make it easier for him . . . She did not know that he was long past being affected by such trifles. If she had dressed in an old sack and painted her face with woad, it would not have altered his obsession, for he believed she loved him.

They reached the door of the cottage, and she hesitated. She did not want to ask him in; but, emboldened by the touch of her hand and the memory of her warm kisses by the river, he opened the wire door and pulled her inside and into his arms.

For a moment she went limp, then she stiffened, her lips rigid and unyielding against his. She tore her mouth away and said, rather unsteadily: 'Aren't you forgetting yourself? What about Maria?'

He looked dazed, then bewildered. 'Maria? But I told you, it's *you* I love. I'm sure Maria knows there's someone else, that—'

'And do you really think I'll remember you once the season is over, and I've gone back to the city?'

'But—but, Mandy, you said—'

'A momentary madness. Goodness knows what I said.' Her voice was steady now, almost hard. 'It was fun, and you are very attractive. But you surely didn't think—'

'You said—you said you could quite understand Desdemona.'

166

'And no doubt she had time to regret her madness before she died. No, Mike, you can surely see that Maria is much more suitable for you . . . the peasant type.'

Mike dropped his arms and stepped back. His face looked greyish with shock.

'In the fairy-stories,' said Mandy, 'the herd-boy always turns out to be a prince in disguise. Can you produce a palace, or even an uncle who is a king? King Billy perhaps! King Billy of the River Murray tribes.' She began to laugh, laughing so that she would not burst into tears at the sight of his face, all the light and confidence gone out of it.

'And I called you a princess,' said Mike wonderingly. 'Do you know what you are? You're just a—a cold-blooded . . .'

'Bitch? I quite agree. But never mind, I won't be here much longer.'

He turned and wrenched the door open, and was gone. She caught one glimpse of his bitter, baffled face as he went past the window. Then she flung herself face-down on her stretcher and lay inert. Misery flooded over her in choking waves.

*　　　*　　　*

There was to be another evening party at the Jordans', to which Pike's Privileged Pickers, or Mitch, Mandy and Maria, had been invited. Maria, however, could not go as she had been invited to a dance by Mike.

Mandy declared that she did not want to go; but Mitch, who had seen Mike's face when he came back from the house that day, and who had found Mandy in bed with her face turned to the wall when

167

she came home in the afternoon, thought the outing would do her good. She was worried about Mandy. She was morose and silent, and her lovely eyes had a cloudy, troubled look and were ringed with deep shadows.

To take her out of herself Mitch suggested that they should go shopping in the afternoon; she for a maternity smock which she would soon be needing, and Mandy for a short evening-dress. Mandy went indifferently, and bought a severely plain dress of black taffeta with a low neckline.

Once more the clink of bottles sounded from the veranda, and a scent of cut grass and roses drifted from the dew-wet garden. But the night was chill, the poplars showed almost bare branches against the starlit sky, where the Milky Way stretched in a curving river of light.

In the big drawing-room there was a fire of vine-roots, a friendly blaze not giving out a great deal of heat. Mandy listlessly accepted a gin-squash from Bob Jordan, whose gallant remarks about her appearance fell for once on deaf ears. Mitch became caught up in a group of women discussing confinements, and found herself for the first time listening with interest to the gruesome details of what she would soon have to suffer. The men drifted towards the table where the bottles were set out, and began telling bawdy stories.

Mandy swallowed her drink without tasting it. She would like to get drunk, to forget everything ... She accepted another drink and swallowed that too, feeling the sharp edge of the pain become dulled, though it was still insistently there, like a toothache which can almost be ignored but which you know will be set raging again if a certain spot is touched.

'Oh, Mike, Mike, Mike!' she murmured into her glass. 'If only you were here! How am I to get through the awful boredom of this night?' She leant despondently on the mantelpiece and gazed unseeingly into the fire.

'—that is Miss Weston, who's staying in our spare cottage. Would you like to meet her?'

Mandy looked up, and became aware of Mrs Jordan bearing down on her with a young man in tow. He was rather small, and lithely built, with a pale face and a thick dark moustache. A pair of lively, alert blue eyes with a gleam of humour in them studied her intently as he crossed the room. She had seen that face before—where?

Mrs Jordan muttered vague introductions and drifted away in a flutter of chiffon. 'I'm sorry—' began Mandy, who was not concentrating very well, about to ask him to repeat his name.

He raised a hand to stop her. '*Why do you always wear mourning?*' he asked.

'*I dress in black to match my life.*'

'Ah! I thought so.' He laughed delightedly. 'I thought you looked like something out of a Chekhov play. Russian ... Slavic, anyway. Tell me, you don't belong here, do you?'

'I'm an Australian, if that's what you mean, and so were my parents. It annoys me rather when people, especially people from overseas, say "But *you're* not Australian, are you?", obviously meaning it as a compliment.'

'As a matter of fact I am from overseas—what you call a Pommy. I came up here to do a locum, and I was amazed. The air—so fresh, so dry, so pure.' He inhaled through delicately quivering

169

nostrils, and his eyes glittered with a kind of feverish energy. 'And the wine—why didn't anybody tell me about it in England? This is an excellent claret,' he raised his glass and passed it under his nose, and the nostrils quivered again.

'What are you drinking? Gin? That's no good for you. I'll get you a decent drink.' He hurried away to fetch a bottle of claret, and Mandy was relieved of the flow of words, the brilliant, penetrating gaze that would not let her be alone with her thoughts. He came back with a clean glass and filled it from the bottle. 'There you are—try that. Doctor's orders.'

'Doctor! Of course! That's where I've seen you before.' Mandy waved the glass at him. 'Don't you remember, they called you when the little boy fell in the channel?'

'Good Lord! You're the girl who did the artificial respiration. I remember now. I noticed your eyes then, but the costume was—well, it didn't reveal your possibilities. Smart girl. You saved the kiddie's life, probably.'

'Oh, I don't know. Anyone could have done it.'

'But no one else did. Now tell me what you're doing here. You don't belong in this town, do you?'

'No, I'm from the city . . .' She found that it was easy to talk to him, he was so eager and receptive. He wanted to hear everything about Australia she could tell him. Time began to flow again, she forgot the insistent ache at her heart. He said that he would be returning to the city soon, and hoped to see her there. Immediately she was reminded that the grape season was almost over, that soon she must leave Vindura, and perhaps never see Mike again. She emptied her glass and turned it upside down on the mantelpiece.

'"Turn down an empty glass,"' he said. 'What does that mean? The finish of something?'

'Perhaps . . . Something already finished.'

'I hope, all the same, that our friendship is only beginning.'

At that her old coquettish spirit flared up again; she raised her lovely, shadowed eyes to his and gave him a long look. He blinked, slightly dazzled, and swallowed the rest of his drink.

'And just when I've discovered you, I have to leave. I've a mid. case due, and I only dropped in for half an hour.'

'But it's quite early yet. I thought babies were always born in the middle of the night.'

'Not *always*, though they often are—inconsiderate little beggars.'

'Don't tell me you're talking about confinements, too,' said Mitch, coming up to them with a glass in her hand. 'I came over here for a change of conversation.'

'It's his job,' said Mandy laconically. 'He brings unfortunate infants into this world of sorrow. Mitch, this is Dr . . . Carlton, is it? Mrs Fairbrother, an expectant mother.'

'Oh, Mandy!' protested Mitch. 'Don't be so clinical. I'm a grape-picker, Dr Carlton. I could write a new chapter in the medical books on Pickers' Hands, a most painful complaint.'

'That's a new one to me. But what unusual names—Mitch and Mandy!'

'My name was Mitchison before I was married. It's easy to remember them—Mitch rhymes with bitch, and Mandy with Candy. Her real name is Miranda.'

171

'I'll remember that!' he laughed, and went away to make his farewells to his hostess.

'Let's go too,' said Mandy, suddenly despondent again.

'We can't! Not yet. Why don't you play something?'

'No!' said Mandy in a violent undertone. 'I feel I never want to touch the piano or sing again.'

CHAPTER TWENTY

And if the Wine you drink, the Lip you press,
End in the Nothing all Things end in—Yes—
Then fancy while Thou art, Thou are but what
Thou Shalt be—Nothing—Thou shalt not be less.

'What's the matter, not eatin' yer good breakfust? Yer must be in love!' Rosie set down the teapot and stood with her hands on her hips, regarding Mandy with a not unfriendly gaze. Now that the season was nearing its end and she was soon to lose her boarders, she began to feel almost an affection for them.

'I'm not hungry,' said Mandy listlessly.

Many a true word is spoken in jest, thought Mitch unhappily, looking at Mandy's shadowed eyes and drooping mouth.

'She has not yet got over the party,' said Maria. 'Ah, that Australian beer! It goes to the head. I was dancing until after midnight, yet I was quite well yesterday morning, and today I am quite well.'

'*Brava!*' said Mitch. 'All those verbs! Your English is certainly coming on.'

'What verbs?'

'The ones you just used—the imperfect, the past perfect, and the present tense.'

'I do not know one tense from another—'

'"I *don't* know." You may not know their names, but you know how to use them correctly.'

'Truly, Mitch? You are not pulling my leg?'

'No, fair dinkum, Maria. You're a real Aussie now.'

Maria beamed at her.

'Well, come on youse girls, if yer want any more. I got to wash up and get stuck into that grape-picking.'

For Rosie had joined the pickers for the last few weeks since they had been working in the vines about her cottage.

'I finished long ago,' said Mandy, getting up and leaving the others to finish their cups of tea. 'See you at the racks.'

Mitch was worried over Mandy; she had not expected her to take her sacrifice so much to heart. But to counteract this there was the obvious, glowing happiness of her other friend. Maria looked quite beautiful this morning, with her usually tranquil face animated and a sparkle of joy in her dark eyes.

On the way back to their own cottage she stopped Mitch with a hand on her arm. 'I want to tell you why I am so happy,' she said. 'He has asked me—on Saturday night, after the dance. When I am married to Mike I will be truly an Australian, *non è vero*?'

'Maria! You beaut! And did you tell him about— you know?'

'Not until afterwards. He did not know, when he

asked me. And then, when I told him, he was so surprised, and pleased, and cross, and gentle . . . I mean he was cross that I did not tell him before. We are to be married soon, as soon as the fruit is in and he is free to go away for a holiday.'

'That's wonderful! I'll have to come up for the wedding. For I'm afraid I promised Richard I'd go home as soon as everything was settled. He'll be coming for me next week-end.'

'I do not—I don't—know how you have stayed away from him for so long.'

'I don't either. Home is where *he* is, whether we've got a house or not. I see that now.'

Maria's heart echoed the words. Home is where *he* is. My home is here . . . Australia is my home. Here is my home . . . And her children and her children's children would be Australians. They would forget that their grandmother came from a little village in Italy; they would go to school, and learn to speak this queer Australian-English as a native tongue: beaut, good-oh, dinkum, orright, so long, crook, bastard . . .

She began to laugh, thinking how casually they dropped that last word into their conversation, in an almost affectionate way: 'He's not a bad old bastard,' or 'Course he's a bastard, but he's not a *silly* bastard, if you know what I mean.' The one thing they didn't mean, she knew now, was that 'he' was the illegitimate son of unmarried parents. She should really not have been so upset at the idea of having a baby.

Mike had been delighted, disbelieving, dismayed, and proud by turns, when she told him. He had asked her to marry him in the car, going home, while he drove with one hand, the other clasping her full breast.

And then, when he stopped the car and kissed her, she had told him, crying a little in her happiness.

'You should have told me,' he kept saying. 'I should have known, I suppose ... But I didn't guess ... I didn't dream ... I've always been scared of marriage and having children, and all that. And now it's just happened. A son to leave my land to, when I get me own vines!'

'But if it is a daughter ...'

'That's all right! We'll have a son next time,' he said, and laughed. 'You must be careful ... I'll see you don't work too hard, next week. Maria! Little mother ...'

*   *   *

The morning was frosty, and the dew so heavy that the vine-leaves were soaking wet, so there was no dust to give Mandy hay-fever. In spite of the clear golden sunlight, the remote and perfect blue sky through which black crows wavered with melancholy cries, it was cold enough for the girls to keep their woollen pullovers on as they picked.

When they had settled into their stride, and the gold and amber sultanas were thudding rapidly into the tins, Mitch plucked up heart to tell Mandy. She said, through the wall of green leaves: 'Maria tells me that Mike has asked her, and they are going to get married as soon as all the fruit is in. She is terribly happy, of course. She doesn't realise what you have done for her. It was really unselfish and good of you, Man.' She stopped and listened. There was absolute stillness on the other side of the

175

vine. No more bunches fell into the tins. 'Mandy? Did you hear what I said?'

'Yes. I heard.'

'I don't know what you said to him, but the reaction evidently sent him straight to Maria. Their baby will be a dinkum Aussie, a brand-new Australian with his roots going back about twenty thousand years. She's had a rotten spin, losing her proxy husband like that, and she had nowhere to go when the season ended. I'm so glad it's all come out right . . . for her.'

There was no answer, so Mitch began to work again. After a while Mandy's voice came through the vine: 'I think I'll have to go up to the cottage.'

'Are you feeling sick?'

'Not exactly. But, as Tennyson put it: "The Curse has come upon me!"'

'Oh, the curse! Didn't you expect it?'

'Of course I did. But not just this morning. I'll have to—oh Lord! Here comes young David.'

'Hullo, Mandy, how many tins you done, Mandy? Is you pickin' sultanas? C'n I help? I've got my pocket-knife wif me.'

Since he had been rescued by Mandy, and his mother had impressed on him what a wonderful person she was, he was always wanting to help her. Mother Mac in her gratitude baked delicious cakes at night after her long day's work, iced them in the morning and brought them to Mandy with apologies: ' 'Fraid the icing's not quite set . . . I know how youse must long for a bit of homemade cake after Rosie Binks's shop slabs . . . It's no trouble, dear, I like to cook.'

'Thank you, Davey,' said Mandy more gently than usual. 'You can go on filling my tins while I'm

176

up at the cottage, will you?'

'Has you got your watz, Mandy? Is your watz broked? What times does it say?'

'Here, you read it yourself. I'll put it on your wrist, see, and tighten the band so you can't lose it. It says half-past ten.'

'Harst-past ten,' said David solemnly, overcome with joy at having this great treasure to himself. 'Oo, gee! C'n I *keep* it?' he breathed.

'Yes, I won't want it.' She went off without a word to Mitch.

It was nearly an hour later when Mitch began to wonder. Half-past ten she had gone, and now it was nearly half-past eleven; in half an hour it would be lunch-time. David ran off to show the watch proudly to his mother. It was odd that Mandy should let him have the watch which she valued so much . . . Mitch laid down her knife and walked up the track.

As she had half-expected, the cottage was deserted. The wire door creaked in the silence. The sunlight fell across the bare wooden floor. Mandy's handbag was lying on her table. She had not gone to town, then, to buy some necessary she'd found she needed. She would hardly go for a walk in her present condition; she had said nothing about not coming back to work, however.

Not coming back! The watch, given so carelessly to David! Mitch shot out of the cottage and began running down to the main channel. She knew Mandy's moodiness and something of her family history, and the morbid interest she had always taken in suicide. Then she paused. No, Mandy was too good a swimmer to choose the channel or the river. There was the railway-line, and the next train

177

was due in about an hour . . . But by now she could be anywhere along the line.

Mitch went to the racks and sought out Mike. By an effort she kept her voice calm. She must not let him know; she must not spoil what Mandy had done for Maria. She said:

'Mike, I have an odd request to make of you. Mandy has gone off in a huff. We had a quarrel, and she tore off, I'm not sure where, probably towards the river, and I'm afraid she'll get lost. Could I take your car and go and look for her? I've been driving since I was sixteen, and I'd be very careful.'

'Of course, Mitch; but she may not keep to any tracks. Don't you think I'd better come?'

'No, I know you're busy, and she can't have gone far. But she's such a moody creature, you don't know what she'll do next. She might go and catch a train back to the city.'

Mike did not particularly want to come; the very sight of Mandy was painful to him now. He said musingly: 'There *is* something odd about her. I remember one night out at the Lock, she spoke very strangely . . . something about her mother.'

'Yes . . . well, can I take it?'

'Go ahead. There's plenty of petrol in the tank.'

'I'll put some in anyway.'

Mitch ran towards the car. The Lock, the Lock! Of course, the place a strong swimmer would choose, the foaming whirlpool below the weir where nothing could keep afloat.

She started the unfamiliar car with difficulty, found the bottom gear and roared off in a cloud of dust. She would drive in along the railway-line, and then ask at the Post Office for the road to the Lock.

178

The line and the road to the town were deserted. As she neared the outskirts of the main streets there were a few vehicles, and under a tree outside someone's gate a small English car was parked. As she drew nearly level she saw a man come out of the gate, a man with a large moustache who carried a small black bag.

She stamped on the brakes and leapt out of the car. 'Dr Carlton! Oh, Doctor, I'm glad I saw you. It's Mandy—she's disappeared, and I'm afraid she's planning to do away with herself. Will you come with me, out to the Lock? We may be too late.'

One glance at her face showed that she was in earnest.

'Hop in, we'll go in my car,' he said at once. 'I thought she had a temperamental Russian look. Has there been some upset since the other night?'

'No—yes, she's been under a strain for some time, and this morning she heard something . . . It doesn't matter. Only hurry.'

They asked the way at the Post Office, and were soon tearing along the road to the Lock.

CHAPTER TWENTY-ONE

Alas, that Spring should vanish with the Rose!
That Youth's sweet-scented Manuscript should
close!
The Nightingale that in the Branches sang,
Ah, whence, and whither flown again, who knows!

Mandy walked down to the corner in a black mood.

She didn't know where she was going, only that she wanted to get away from everyone and be miserable in peace.

She stopped at the railway-line and stared at the rails, polished, gleaming like water, as they disappeared into a perspective point in the distance. Here was a way out. Either she would catch the evening train to the city, or she would throw herself under it; but she couldn't go back to face Maria's happiness.

She had picked up her purse and put it in her jeans pocket without any plan. Now, as a bus came along the main road, she hailed it and got aboard. She noticed nothing of the passing vines, the willows that dropped yellow leaves into the main channel. Her eyes were turned broodingly inward.

What hurt most was that Mike had given her up so easily, had turned so instantly to Maria. She had thought he would be downcast and inconsolable for a time; she could have borne a gaze of sorrowful reproach, but not the light, jaunty, almost jeering tone he had adopted this morning. He had looked at her with positive aversion. And this of course was what she had wanted.

Nevertheless she felt she had succeeded too well. He believed she cared nothing for him, and pride made him act as if she did not exist. He was not one to cry for the moon.

Well, once she was dead he would understand her true feelings, and remember her with tenderness. It was this rather childish wish to be thought well of by Mike which drove her to thoughts of suicide. 'Even Mitch doesn't understand how I feel,' she thought. Tears of self-pity gathered in her eyes. She dashed them away, and got out of the bus in the town.

Walking down towards the river, she considered swimming out and then along the centre of the stream until she was exhausted. It would be pleasant rather than frightening, just to let her tired legs drop, and sink down among the grey-green depths. But she could swim so well, perhaps the will to live would be too strong for her.

She stopped by the big hotel on the river frontage. She would just go and have a drink first; she had hours to wait for the evening train. She ordered a gin-squash from the young, dark-haired waiter who seemed to be the only person about. She knew him by sight; they had sometimes dropped in for a beer on a Saturday afternoon in the lounge, for the bar was forbidden to women. The waiter's name was Feathers, and the other waiters called him Chook.

'Not workin' today?' asked Chook with easy familiarity, glancing at her grape-picking clothes.

'Not today. I'm on strike. I'm celebrating,' she said with a crooked smile, 'the end of the season—for me.'

'Good for you. A one-girl strike, eh?'

'That's right. The others are still working—the scabs.'

She swallowed her drink as soon as it came, tasting the gin unmixed in the bottom of the glass. After the second gin-squash her legs felt weak. She was not used to drinking in the morning. But it helped her not to think . . .

'A double whisky!' she said recklessly when Chook came back again for her empty glass. He raised his eyebrows, which were very thick and black and met right across his nose. He scooped up

181

her glass, however, with an expert sweep of the hand.

'When he came back with the whisky he said: 'These things ain't made with water, you know.'

'I know, Chooky-hen. You won't have to carry me out. I'm a confirm—I'm a hardened drinker.'

'Yair. But you don't wanter go ruinin' that schoolgirl complexion.'

He wiped up the spill marks on the table, his lank black hair falling over one eye, and went and stood by the glass doors. She began to be irritated by the anxious, almost motherly looks he kept directing at her to see if she meant to drink any more.

At last she got up and weaved her way with dignity among the tables, over the thick carpet, to the door marked 'Ladies'. There seemed to be more tables than before, and the space between them was smaller, but she made it without a collision.

*　　　*　　　*

Mitch and Dr Carlton stood and stared at the foaming weir, and the water trickling through the closed Lock gates. There was not a soul in sight. Half-unwillingly they walked out above the spillway and looked down at the churning water. No dark shape bobbed among the foam.

Relieved, they went back to the car. 'We'd better inform the police,' said the doctor. 'They'll make a proper search . . .'

'Oh no! Not the police. They may be nothing to worry about, really.' Mitch felt she could not bear to see them solemnly dragging the river.

'But you said she has these moods, this impulse

182

towards self-destruction. What about the train-line?'

'There's no train before this evening.'

'Well, that's good, anyway.'

They drove slowly round the town, seeing no sign of Mandy; then decided to go back the other way and take the track out to the river and the picnic-place. Dr Carlton was surprised to note the depth of his relief at not finding her in the river. He took more than a professional interest in the missing girl. What lovely, alluring eyes she had! There must be a great deal behind them: a mind that it would be fascinating to explore. And her coolness and resource in saving that child's life . . . He trod impatiently on the accelerator.

*   *   *

Mandy noticed that the floor of the washroom undulated gently in front of her as she walked. She sat down and concentrated until the up-and-down movement ceased. Her head felt light as a dry puff-ball. Already the pain of Mike's engagement was dulled, she no longer felt the need to cry out and beat her head against something hard.

The picture of herself being found dead on the train-line had faded a little (would that nice young doctor do the post-mortem? She hoped not), and the other picture of a remorseful Mike lifting her broken body in his arms. After all, she was not a very romantic figure in her stained denim jeans and cotton work-shirt. Anna Karenina, she felt, would have managed things much better.

And what was she going to do until the beastly train arrived? It was rather hard to be a tragic heroine in a little country town where there were only about two trains a day.

She was going to feel terrible when the effects of the gin and the whisky wore off, and she couldn't sit drinking all day under Chook's anxious eye. She decided to get a bottle of wine and take it down by the river for the rest of the afternoon.

She walked carefully to the bottle department and bought some strong, sweet muscat. Then she wandered down the sloping lawns and sat under an ornamental shrub close to the river-bank, and forced herself to take a long drink from the bottle. She put the cork back and lay down under the bush. The sun came through the leaves in sudden sharp gleams that hurt her eyes. It was well past noon and she'd had nothing to eat since breakfast, but she didn't feel hungry. The important thing was not to think. She sat up and took another swig from the bottle.

There was something infinitely soothing about the broad sweep of river in front, the willows softly cascading their fountains of green from the opposite shore, and the quiet, invisible flow of water held back by the lock and weir.

The Lock! She sat up so suddenly that her head throbbed. Why hadn't she thought of it before? The place where she had stood and looked over at the mad, churning water on that night—it seemed years ago—when Mike had pulled Mitch out of the river. Mike's voice: 'There'd not be much hope for anyone who fell in there.' Oh Mike, darling Mike! But she mustn't think; she'd have one more drink to give her courage, and then she would walk out to the weir. It was so much less messy than the railway-line, and not so unpleasant for other people.

Mandy was not given to unselfish thinking, but now she began to consider other people besides herself and Mike. There was Mitch, who would be dreadfully upset certainly, but she had Richard to comfort her. And then there was her father.

She hadn't given a thought to her father, that lonely figure; he had been so remote from her inner life for so long. But how different he might have been, how gay and companionable, but for the tragedy in his life! He had never been a happy man since she had known him. And was she to put this further burden upon him; to make him feel that he had failed both his wife and his daughter? It would be so cruel.

She got up, steadying herself against the sturdy shrub which had half concealed her. The bottle, half-empty, rolled along the ground. She heard carefully-modulated voices nearby, and turned to see Mr and Mrs Pike escorting a toothy female in smartly-cut clothes, a small feathered hat, and just the right amount of lipstick for her age. She was evidently a visitor to the town, and they were showing her round.

'These gardens are a community effort entirely,' Mr Pike was saying in his pompous, public-meeting voice. (What voice did he use when he was in bed with his wife, Mandy wondered fleetingly, or did he address her like a hall-full of people too?)

'Chawming,' said the visitor. 'A chawming little town altogether. And the hotel is a community one too? Of course, in England . . .'

She stopped in mid-sentence as Mandy appeared before her on the path: mud to the ankles, hair wild and full of leaves, her shirt stained with grape-juice and dust.

'Why, Mr Pike!' said Mandy in her most seductive tones. 'How *do* you do? We have seen so little of you lately, and I did want to thank you for your chawming hostility—I mean hospitality. I have seldom inhabited a more delightfully appointed hut. Such comfort and convenience!'

The look of dazed shock on Mr Pike's flabby face was like a tonic to her. In a sudden reaction to her grim mood of depression, Mandy felt a wild flow of spirits. The visiting lady's eyebrows had shot up so far that they were lost under her hat-brim, and Mrs Pike was rapidly turning puce. Her horrified gaze was fixed on the half-empty wine-bottle which lay on the path. She clutched her husband's arm and hissed: 'Do you mean to say you know this— this—?'

'Yes, yes,' he muttered. 'I told you, you remember? Her father is a great friend of Walton's... Er, may I present Miss Weston, Lady Halibury? Miss Weston, my wife, Mrs Pike.'

'How do you do?' said Mandy sweetly. Her half-offered hand was not taken. 'Lady Halibury, you must come and see our humble abode. It will be quite an experience for you. A unique experience. Thick, white cups with cracks in, no saucers, canvas stretchers to sleep on, and nowhere to hang your clothes except on nails in the wall. Have you ever slept in grey blankets, Lady Halibury? They tickle the nose, but they're warmer than sheets. On hot nights, of course, we don't wear anything at all...'

'Edward! This young woman is drunk. Come, Lady Halibury, let us return to the car. I really must apologise—'

'Not at all,' said Mandy, enunciating her words with elaborate care but swaying slightly on her feet, 'if you imagine, Mrs Pike, that I am under the influence of alcohol, I can assure you that you are labouring under a delusion. I am, in fact, cold, stone, stinking sober.'

'Miss Weston! I beg you—you are in no fit state...' Mr Pike stepped forward impulsively and on to the empty bottle, which rolled under his foot. With a graceful slide he landed in the river. He was so taken by surprise that he did not even cry out as he disappeared with a resounding splash.

'Oh dear! Oh dear! He'll be drowned, I know!' wailed Mrs Pike. 'With those heavy boots on, and he can scarcely swim!'

'Never fear, Madam. Your husband shall not drown,' said Mandy dramatically, kicking off her shoes and diving neatly into the river. The bank was steep; Mr Pike had sunk in twelve feet of water. She caught him by the collar as he came up, and in this undignified fashion towed him to the bank. Mrs Pike was stretching her hand to help him, regardless of muddy splashes on her nylon stockings and suede shoes. The grim-looking old trout was actually fond of him, thought Mandy.

Poor Mr Pike had all the pompousness washed out of him for the present. His hair was glued in sorry strands about his bald patch, the wet clothes clung to his rotund figure and turned him into a comic caricature of himself.

But Mandy when wet looked particularly attractive, with her golden mermaid-hair and sodden shirt transparently outlining her lovely breasts, and her eyes washed to a clear green.

Or so Dr Carlton thought, hurrying down the

slope of the lawns with Mitch behind him. They had come back to the centre of the town after a fruitless drive out to the river, and were on their way to the police station to report Mandy's disappearance, when they saw the tableau on the bank opposite the hotel.

Dr Carlton grasped Mr Pike's wet hand and shook it gratefully. 'We've been looking everywhere for her,' he said. 'Did you pull her out, sir?'

'No! She pulled *me* out. I slipped on a blasted bottle—where is it? It must have gone into the water. I'd have been all right, of course,' he added hastily. 'But thank you all the same, Miss, er—Miss Weston.'

'A very neat rescue,' said Lady Halibury crisply.

'Yes!' said Mrs Pike resentfully, 'but he wouldn't have fallen in if it hadn't been for her.'

They went back to their car, Mr Pike squelching as he walked.

'Oh, Man! We were so worried.' Mitch had taken Mandy's hand, and in one quick, reassuring squeeze all was understood between them. Dr Carlton was looking at Mandy with twinkling eyes.

'You seem to make a habit of saving lives. As that is my profession too, I think we should see more of each other.'

Mandy smiled. In her large, strange-coloured eyes was that indefinable invitation of promise which had made so many masculine hearts beat faster. 'Well, will you begin by driving us back to the cottage? I must get out of these wet things.'

'I have to drive Mike's car back, if you'd take me to it,' said Mitch. 'You bring Mandy; though she doesn't look as if she needed medical attention.'

188

'Oh, I don't know; shock and immersion . . .'

'It's poor old Pikelet who had the shock, I fancy. But I'm afraid I don't look respectable enough for the main street of Vindura.'

'You look absolutely wonderful,' said Denver Carlton sincerely.

Back in the hut, Mandy peeled off her wet clothes and rubbed herself dry. 'That doctor is rather a dear,' she said. 'He's so interested in everything, so fizzing with energy and appreciation, you can't help liking him. And I thought the English were supposed to be cold and reserved.'

'There are exceptions, no doubt. I hate those vague generalisations about people. You might as well say all Australians are slovenly dressers and talk through their noses.'

'Yes; it's just as silly. Throw me my pyjamas, will you? I think I'll just crawl into bed and have a snooze. I've had a tremendous amount to drink, you know. I'd better sleep it off.'

'Then I'll leave you quiet. Sure you're all right?'

'Quite sure. And Mitch—thank you for coming after me.'

'That's all right, mate. Don't mention it.'

Mitch closed the wire door softly after her, and went back to work. She told Mike that she had found Mandy in the town, that they had made up their quarrel, but she would not be coming back to work today.

'That's all right with me,' said Mike. 'She's on piecework, anyway. She doesn't have to worry about the money, does she?'

'No; too much money has perhaps been bad for Mandy. You mustn't judge her too harshly, Mike.

She—'

'I don't presume to judge her at all. She's outside my comprehension.'

She left it at that. It was evident that Mike had not recovered from the blow to his pride.

*　　　*　　　*

Mandy lay with her face turned to the wall, as she had on the night when Maria followed Mike into the storm; but now she felt strangely indifferent. She was too drowsy to think or to care. She felt the comfort of the rough grey blanket that she drew over her face, shutting out the light, and the comfort of Mitch's sturdy friendship. She was glad she had not done anything to hurt Mitch, who understood everything without the need for explanations. She would go home and try to be a companion to her father, if it was not too late; she intended never to marry.

When she woke it seemed only minutes later, yet a mellowing of the light, the feel of the sunny day, told her that the afternoon was well advanced. Her first thought was that she did not want Maria to find her prostrated; she got up quickly and went over to the house for a hot bath, then dressed and did her face carefully. When she heard the others approaching, she was able to turn towards the door with a casual smile.

'Well, I played hookey—I mean I took the day off, Maria,' she said. 'Don't tell Mike, will you? Did Mitch tell you about it?'

'*Si*, Mandy.'

'And she tells me that you and ... Mike are engaged. Congratulations. The best woman won.

That is, the best for Mike.'

'Oh, I do not know ... But thank you, very much.'

'*Prego*, my child.'

The others went across for their bath, while Mandy sat down and lit a cigarette with a hand which was not quite steady. Her mouth was dry, her head ached, and she felt a longing for another drink.

*   *   *

'This is our last expedition together!' said Mitch rather sorrowfully, as the three girls walked down the drive to catch the bus on the following Saturday afternoon. Richard was arriving that night, and she would be driving home with him in the morning.

By the end of the week the season would be finished. Mandy would return to the city, and Maria go to board with an Italian family in the town until the day of her wedding.

'Let's have a real shopping spree!' said Mandy. 'I want to get a wedding present for Maria, and a boy's watch for David' (for his mother had made him return the good watch, much to his sorrow), 'and something for Mother Mac, and a bottle of plonk for Rosie. Oh, and a new dress for me.'

'*Another* new dress! *Mamma mia*!'

'Yes, I am going out somewhere rather special tonight. Dr Carlton is calling for me after he's finished consulting.'

Mandy looked rather smug, and Mitch wondered again at the change in her friend. Her expression was softer, she seemed to have mellowed in some way. The experience of working on the land had been good for her—or was it just that she was older? They were all indefinably older, changed, a new self growing out of their old selves as imperceptibly as a plant put on leaves or a flower unfolded.

Maria was more Madonna-like than ever, her pale olive brow serene and lovely under its cloud of dark hair. Since she was *promessa*, with the status of a wife-to-be, she had a new dignity and assurance. And as for herself—Mitch looked wryly down at her waistline—today the zip-fastener on her dress had simply refused to meet, and she'd had to cover the space with a wide belt.

And Richard would be here tonight. He had sounded pleased and excited on the telephone. 'I have a surprise for you—a pleasant surprise—a very pleasant surprise,' he'd said, and would say no more. She guessed that it was about a house. She didn't mind if it was a year before they could move in, as long as she had something to look forward to. Living in one room with two fellow-workers had taught her something about living with others.

Dead, pale-brown leaves were whirled across the drive by a sharp breeze. Two nights ago there had been a severe frost that withered the remaining leaves on the vines. The next day a strong wind rose, and the air was thick with fallen leaves. Today the vines were almost bare.

Mitch was disappointed. She remembered the lovely autumn vineyards she had seen in the south, burning through the mists in gold and russet and amber for a month or more. Here were no mellow lingerings of a declining year; withered age came at one stroke.

The poplars were like witches' brooms, mere

bundles of sticks against the sky, that for once was grey and overcast. Mitch looked back at the house and the two cottages.

They appeared bare and mean, reduced to ordinariness without their surrounding verdure. Only the gum trees by the dam retained their leaves and their original pride and grace.

It was sad to see all else so changed. She remembered the day they had driven in the gate with Mr Pike and first seen this place, and the strange feeling she'd had of an eternal moment among the flux of time. It seemed long ago now. So much had happened since then.

She had the sensation of standing on a sandbank which felt firm, yet was being eaten away and undermined by relentless waters. You could not hold the moment, which was forever fleeting. This day was being swept away into the past with all the others already gone. She would begin to look back upon it: 'When I was at Vindura ... last year, grape-picking on the Murray ... When I was a girl ... Once, long ago ...'

'Let's sing something,' she said, shaking off her thoughts, feeling the present fall into place and close firmly about her with an almost audible click. 'Mandy, you begin.'

Mandy was thinking about the train journey from the city, when they had met Maria. She sang:

'*Ah quant'è bella giovenezza*
Che si fugge tuttavia—'

'Oh, for Pete's sake! Not that!'
'Then I will sing,' said Maria. 'Listen:

Non ti scordar di me . . .

That means, Mitch: "Do not forget me".'

'I won't forget, Maria. I'll never forget the time we all spent here.'

'Nor I,' said Mandy, thinking of Mike.

'Me also,' said Maria.

Photoset, printed and bound in Great Britain by
REDWOOD BURN LIMITED, Trowbridge, Wiltshire

Also available in Windsor Large Print

BARBARA TAYLOR BRADFORD
A Woman of Substance

One of the richest women in the world, ruler of a business empire stretching from Yorkshire to the glittering cities of America and the rugged vastness of Australia, Emma Harte is truly 'A Woman of Substance'. But what price has she paid?

PHYLLIS A. WHITNEY
Domino

Laurie Morgan's life in New York is haunted by childhood memories she can never quite name. She knows only that the reality of her memories would threaten her very sanity.

SHEILA HOLLAND
A Woman of Iron

Joss Colby was part of the revolution that would make the British iron industry the leader of the world. Only one person—lowly kitchen maid Hannah Noble—stood between him and his possession of the ironworks he coveted.

Windsor Large Print books are stocked by most libraries. If you would like to receive details of other titles in the range please write to:
Department CD,
Chivers Press,
Windsor Bridge Road,
Bath BA2 3AX.